# DEATHICS

# DEATHICS

## A Margaret Binton Mystery

# RICHARD BARTH

ST. MARTIN'S PRESS
NEW YORK

DEATHICS

Design by Dawn Niles

Library of Congress Cataloging-in-Publication Data

Barth, Richard
        Deathics / Richard Barth.
                p.   cm.
        "A Thomas Dunne Book."
        ISBN 0-312-08764-0
        I. Title.
    PS3552.A755D44    1993
    813'.54—dc20                                    92-41156
                                                       CIP

First edition: March 1993

10 9 8 7 6 5 4 3 2 1

*Dedicated To Allen, Amy, And Daniel*

# DEATHICS

# 1

The smoked-salmon wars had heated up and everyone on the benches was having a field day. Zabar's was always doing something exciting to keep the steady flow of food buyers marching through their doors, but never had Margaret Binton seen such a bloodbath of price letting. The word hit the street on Monday, May tenth, that western nova was going down to five-and-a-half dollars a quarter pound, which was a dollar less than normal, and more than seventy-five cents less than Greengrass's price. Not to be outdone, young Gary Greengrass bit the bullet and dropped his price to match Zabar's, hoping that he had staved off a further round of price cuts.

All would have been well if the manager of Murray's Sturgeon Shop, four blocks away on Broadway, hadn't run scared at the minor price adjustment and seen in it visions of another thirties gas-price war. There could be no other explanation why he dropped his price down to the five-dollar level, which was all that was needed to open the floodgates. When all the slashing was over on May fourteenth, western nova was down to $2.80 a quarter, which was the lowest it had been since the Kaiser invaded the Balkans.

As disastrous as this was for the respective owners of the Upper West Side's famous appetizing emporia, it delighted everyone who had ever stood on line with a little numbered ticket in hand, waiting patiently to buy smoked fish. $2.80 a quarter! Unheard of. That week there was such a run on bagels at H and H that they had to get in an extra crew to work a graveyard shift. $2.80 a quarter. . . . at that price everyone stocked up, including Margaret Binton, who bought a pound-and-a-half and squirreled it away in her refrigerator. Of all her friends, she had done the best, waiting patiently as the price filtered down, watching as first Sid ($3.90), then Rena ($3.35), then Berdie ($3.05), made purchases ahead of her. Later on they heard that for one short hour on the fifteenth, Murray's had lowered it to $2.75 before they all came to their senses and brought things back to normal. But by then, New York's Upper West Side had been given a rare and bounteous windfall, and everyone was appreciative.

Margaret couldn't help basking in the glory of her near-perfect timing. For years Sid had been preaching to everyone on the Broadway benches just how miraculous a stock picker he was. "Timing was everything" he always said, and here he had jumped in on the great nova war more than a dollar too soon. No one, not even Rose Gaffery, let him forget it. For a woman who spent most of her day looking through and collecting garbage, Rose had a surprising command of high finance.

"Three-ninety a quarter," she said, smirking. "That's close to a thirty percent premium. If you was buying stocks like that you'd push the Dow Jones over four thousand easy." She spread herself out expansively on the wooden bench and arranged her various shopping bags around her. Even though her clothes were cast-off garments, layered in the most preposterous color scheme, they were all clean. Where she performed this miracle of laundering was the great mystery of the Eighty-second Street benches, but not once had any of the half-dozen or so friends dared to ask. "Personally," she continued, "if I had some money I'd give it to Margaret to invest for me. I'm sure she'd do something smart with it. Options or something."

Sid laughed. "On what, empty pop bottles and beer cans?" He looked over at her lumpy bags. "Or maybe on broken umbrellas. How many broken umbrellas you got now, Rose? Enough to build another *Spirit of St. Louis,* I'll bet."

"No reason to get testy," Berdie said, "just because you jumped in too soon at Zabar's." She reached over and patted Sid's houndstooth jacket sleeve to make the point. Then she sat back, opened a brown paper bag, and started scattering bread crumbs at her feet. Immediately a flock of pigeons flew down from their perches on nearby railings and limbs. Broadway pigeons, everyone knew, were as opportunistic as Wall Street arbitrageurs, and knew exactly where and when to be somewhere. The Eighty-second Street island at 11:45 had been implanted in generations of pigeon genes ever since Berdie Mangione started feeding them ten years before. Stores, restaurants—even banks—came and went on the avenue, but Berdie was as ever present as the scraggly acanthus trees that snaked up through the subway gratings to give some color to the gritty islands of Broadway. Sid looked disgustedly at the scraggly birds rummaging at his feet and cursed.

"Course, it's none of my business, now," Berdie continued, "but I think Margaret's so smart she could get paid for giving advice." She looked over at her friend and winked. Durso, the retired junior high school English teacher and local resident scholar, caught the subtle gesture and raised an eyebrow.

"Mrs. Mangione, your attempts at flattery are as light-handed as your supplicants are well mannered." He nodded down at the birds. "We all know that Margaret's advice is well-founded, but getting paid . . . now that's stretching things just a bit, don't you think?"

3

"Not at all," Berdie said, flushing. "In fact, if you want to know . . ."

Margaret leaned forward and shook her head to stop her friend from continuing. But it was too late. Berdie had the wind up, annoyed at Durso's offhand comment about her birds.

"Margaret's going to be a lawyer." She looked around proudly at her friends on the bench. Besides Sid, Durso, and Rose, there was also Pancher, the part-time superintendent from one of the buildings on the side street, Roosa, trying his best to air out yet another night of Gallo red, and Rena Bernstein, forever connected to her battered Sony Walkman like an infant to a pacifier. As noisy as the street traffic was, the eight old-timers were caught in a silence as deep as if a bell jar had been placed over them. Margaret sat back and sighed as seven pair of eyes focused on her. A guilty expression crossed her lined face.

"What's this?" Sid asked finally. "A joke, surely."

"No joke," Berdie said. "Ask her."

"A lawyer?" Sid chuckled. "You sure the word isn't pronounced 'loiterer'?"

"Very funny," Margaret said with asperity and got up. No one would ever accuse Margaret of being overweight, but of the two styles of older women physiques, she definitely did not fit into the spinsterish, tall and thin category. "Healthy" would be a term used to describe her by someone with a gift for euphemism. Yet she moved with the agility of a younger woman when she wanted to, and right then she gave the impression she wanted to. She walked to the edge of the island, took a deep, indignant breath, and waited for the light to change. However, by the time the cars came to a stop she had second thoughts. She looked at her watch and saw that it was still too early to pick up her little charge, Peter Frangapani, for his Tuesday Cub Scout meeting. That wasn't until school let out at three, so she turned, gave the neat gray-hair bun that was her rear guard an unneeded straightening, and walked back to stand in front of Sid.

4

"For your information, Mr. Rossman, I am merely taking an evening course down at NYU on law and ethics. I don't suppose you'd know what that means, because if you did you might not be so insensitive." She looked down at him with sharp eyes that quite often in the past had made him squirm. But now he was riding too high on a crest of sarcasm to be affected by a simple glare.

"Surely, Margaret, at seventy-two you can't be thinking of a career change?"

"For God's sakes, Sidney, it's just one course."

"But you told me you'd take some more if you liked it," Berdie said. "And that you could get a start on a degree. . . ."

"If I liked it," Margaret added. "And a degree is," she hesitated, "well, it's a long way away. It's nice that you're so positive, Berdie. Too bad it's not catching around here." She took another step and sat back down on the bench.

Roosa groaned and sat up straighter. His face looked like a condensed map of the New York subway and bus system, with all the routes and subroutes represented by networks of abused subcutaneous veins. Roosa had been drinking a quart of wine a day since he was thirty-eight, and trying to make a living selling trim items in New York's garment district. That added up to almost forty years of faithful addiction in which time he had mostly made peace with all the little aches and pains of ill health, as well as all the embarrassments and frustrations of failed business opportunities. "Roosa the Juicer" he had become known to all his clients, and it was as "the Juicer" that he lost all their business.

"Ethics, huh. And lawyers." He snorted. "For my money you could shoot them all and do everyone a big favor."

"And precisely what bad things have lawyers done to you, Mr. Roosa, except get you out of jail every time you need to sleep in a warm place when you can't see straight enough to get home. And for free, I might add." Margaret opened her handbag angrily and rummaged inside a few seconds. The little exchange with Sid and Roosa had gotten her annoyed enough to seek the comfort of a cigarette, only her third of the day.

"Hey, I thought you were trying to stop," Berdie said.

"Real easy with you bunch." Margaret found her pack of Camels and laboriously unwound the rubber band and sheet of paper covering it. Then she drew out a tiny pencil from inside the pack and made a notation on the paper.

"I am putting down that this is a 'stress cigarette.' Compared to 'pleasure cigarettes' these are the hardest to give up." She looked around accusingly. "We are told it takes a lot of cooperation from your friends. Failing that, we are told to remove ourselves from stressful situations." She noted the time of day on the sheet of paper, then wrapped everything up and dropped it back in her handbag. "Which I, of course, could do by simply taking myself off to the Florence Bliss Center." She snapped her handbag shut, stood up again, and fished around in the pocket of her coat.

"Need a light?" Sid said appeasingly and leaned forward. He flicked a lighter and held the flame out to her. "Come on, sit back down, Margaret. We apologize."

"We do?" Roosa grumbled.

Sid gave him a nasty look and reached higher with the flame. Margaret hesitated for only a moment, then leaned forward, lit her cigarette, and sat back down.

"Thank you," she said. "It's nice to know there's a spark of politeness left around here." She inhaled deeply and smiled. Then she took another puff, greedy for the relief the smoke gave her. "You know," she continued, "when Oscar died after we were married for thirty-five years, I had the hardest time giving up all the little rituals we did together, the Sunday walks in Riverside Park, the bridge evenings we had with friends. It was very difficult. But nothing, absolutely nothing, compares with trying to give up these things. I read somewhere that it is a worse addiction than heroin."

Berdie threw out another handful of crumbs. "Is that

6

group you joined helping? What's it called, Smoke Stop-pers?"

"I guess it depends on how many stress situations I find myself in," she said pointedly. "But there is one nice feature of the program: Everyone has a buddy who is also trying to stop, someone to call in case of an emergency. It's very supportive, except . . ."

"Except . . ." Rose prompted.

Margaret chuckled. "Except my buddy's never around."

"What's he do?" Sid said. "Drive a cab?"

"No, he's a writer."

"So, writers are always at home, glued to their typewriters like convicts to their cells, pale, goggle-eyed."

"Not this one. He's always out somewhere. Doing research or something. I never got that part straight." She laughed and took another drag on the Camel. "Once I got him home. I remember I was having a particularly hard time with the Sunday crossword puzzle. There was this one word. . . . I kept stealing glances at the phone, debating whether to call the *Times* help line or not—which I've never done, I want you to know—but it was so unnerving that I just grabbed for my pack. Then I remembered Adrian, so I gave him a try instead and he picked up. And you know what, it worked."

"What did he say to keep you from smoking?" Berdie asked.

"He gave me the word."

Roosa snorted. "That's still cheating."

"I didn't pay for it."

"His name's Adrian?" Berdie asked.

"Yes, he's a very nice young man. I only go to the group once a week, but he's always there. Very conscientious."

"But never home," Sid added.

Margaret shrugged. "But that's going to change. He told me last week he's going to start writing soon. Told me his research was almost finished."

"Good, so we can expect you'll be an ex-smoker by the

end of the month?'' Sid said. There was a trace of sarcasm in his voice.

"I do hope so,'' Margaret said and took a long, leisurely drag on her cigarette. "After this there's only acupuncture left.''

# 2

Peter Frangapani and his mother lived in Margaret's building on West Eighty-second Street. Margaret had gotten to know them over the four years since they had moved in, first by simple politeness in the hallways and lobby, then later in more extended conversations downstairs in the shared basement laundry. Peter was a small, engaging boy of seven-and-a-half who, amongst other things, knew the capitals of all the New England states and the batting averages of every second baseman in the National League. He was something of a wonder to Margaret, who rarely got to speak to children unless they happened to call for a book from her volunteer book cart, which she diligently pushed around Metropolitan Hospital every Thursday. For some unknown reason, Peter had taken a special liking to Margaret. Perhaps because he had never known his real grandparents, perhaps because Margaret was a wonderful listener when he told her all about his yearning to become the first major league left-handed second baseman from P.S. 142. He never failed, at least two nights a week, to run down the hallway, knock on her door, and recount some little fact of baseball minutia he had just read. Her part of the deal was to slip him a cookie or two. This association after a while led Margaret into a friendship with Peter's mother, a modest woman, divorced and struggling with the rigors of raising her son alone in New York City on a schoolteacher's salary. Margaret was as supportive as she could be, so when it turned out that Peter's after-school Cub Scouts meeting was changed to Tuesday, the one day Peter's mom was busy at that hour, Margaret naturally had stepped in. Her offer to pick him up at school and bring him to the church where the meeting was held, then wait and bring him home, was gratefully accepted. Peter had screamed in delight when he was told the good news. At first it was to be an experiment, but the arrangement had worked out so well that by the middle of May the two of them had gotten it down to a regular routine.

This day, Margaret left her friends on the benches precisely at two forty-five and arrived at the door to P.S. 142 just as the children in the second grade were being released. This transition, from the world of smoked fish and Social Security to Nintendo and bubble gum never failed to amuse her. The price comparisons and complaints were almost interchangeable; different products, that was all. Sid's constant diatribe against the prices of new movies sounded very much like Peter's annoyance over the cost of the new Super Mario Bros. III. When she got there he was already wearing his uniform shirt, the sine qua non of an afternoon at Scouts. He grabbed her hand, turned his back proudly on his civilian companions, and the two of them set out uptown.

"You smoke too much," Peter said after a few blocks. "I've been noticing. My den leader says it's a bad habit. Especially for kids to be around. He called it Bambi end fumes."

"Not you too? Come on, Peter. It's not nice to criticize your elders."

The little boy thought about that for a moment. "But that's not fair. Just about everyone is my elders." They

10

walked a few more steps together. "Did Bambi smoke?" he asked with concern.

"Not that I know of. I think the word he was using is 'ambient,' a-m-b-i-e-n-t. It means 'completely surrounding,' like the air." She shook her head. "I bet your den leader has some of his own vices, not the least of which I suspect is intolerance."

"What's a vice?" Peter asked.

"Something that makes you feel good." She leaned closer. "The problem is, it usually makes other people feel bad."

Peter frowned. "You mean like candy bars. My mom is always feeling bad about my candy bars. On Halloween she goes crazy."

"Like candy bars," Margaret agreed. They walked a few minutes more, occasionally stopping to poke their noses into some stores. When they turned the corner and headed towards the big stone church, Peter asked another question.

"If vices make you feel good, why are they bad?"

"Who said they were bad?"

"Oh?" Now Peter's face took on an expression of total confusion. But Margaret didn't care. That's the chance you take, she figured, if you allow your kids to hang around with old people. They might become cynics and counterbalance the high-tone seriousness of all the den leaders of the world. Ambient fumes, indeed!

"Well, here we are," she said. They pushed through a set of doors into the church and followed a half-dozen other Scouts into the basement. "What are you guys doing today?" Margaret asked.

"Knots, I think. Or maybe fire prevention. You know that most fires start because of careless cigarettes?"

"Lay off, Peter." She gave him a dirty look. "Be nice."

"See you later," he said and bounced after his friends. Margaret went up to the waiting room with a smile on her face. He did it to her every time. And the best part, not a stress cigarette in sight.

11

# 3

The classroom she was seated in later that night was overheated and full of anxious students with cold coffee containers and wet overcoats. Law and Ethics met every Tuesday evening regardless of the weather. It was just everyone's misfortune that this, the eighth meeting, was being held on a night when New York's reservoirs were finally getting some much needed replenishment. The course was being given in a room as modern as you could make in a building built back at the turn of the century. There were retro-fitted fluorescent lights, large Formica seminar tables, and walls painted in colors that hadn't been invented until the seventies. Gone were the oak wainscoting panels with incised initials of Margaret's youth, the maps on the wall of the 48 United States, the inkwells, and hinged desktops. Margaret had graduated from Public School 124 back in 1939, at a time when schools looked like what they were, institutions.

The first evening she had walked into LL41 she had been pleasantly surprised by the surroundings, and also by the other dozen or so people that had gathered nervously around the large tables. She had expected to be thrown in with a bunch of young law students, all wearing three-piece suits from Barneys or two-piece suits from Bendel's. What greeted her, however, was the proverbial New York melting pot, and it was a gumbo of particularly long standing. One of the other students was a sixty-year-old man with a yarmulke and white beard who looked as if he would have been more at home in the jewelry district than in Greenwich Village. Another woman was black, appeared to be in her late thirties, and came to every class meeting in a dashiki. Then there were two Russian cab drivers, one Czech computer repair man, and a strange little Chinese student who claimed to be working on a cure for cancer. But everyone seemed to have a great interest in the subject of the class and in their teacher, a man who reminded Margaret of an aging Robert Preston of *The Music Man*. He had the same command of his listeners and the same showmanship as a good carny. And he directed the class like a superb conductor, bringing up the volume in one area, clarifying a line from another. The fact that he was talking about law and not about music did little to dispel Margaret's notion that she was being played upon like an instrument. But as far as she was concerned, there was nothing like a good puzzle, whether it was in a crossword, a riddle, or in the maze of sometimes ambiguous legal principles that were being paraded before them every Tuesday night. That particular evening they were discussing what their teacher, Professor William Guyers, referred to as the classic buried bodies case. *People v. Garrow.*

In 1974, a Mr. Garrow had been indicted on a murder charge. In discussing the case with their client, the two defense attorneys, Mesrs. Armani and Belge, found out from Garrow that he had committed two other, unrelated, murders and had hidden the bodies in a nearby state park. The bodies of the young victims had as yet not been discovered, and the parents of the victims were still in doubt as to what had happened to their children. Belge went to the location, discovered and photographed the bodies. At a later date, rather than disclose this information, Armani and Belge tried to broker their knowledge of the two other unsolved murders to the DA in a strategy to plea-bargain their client, Garrow's, current problem. Unfortunately for them and Garrow, the ploy didn't work and he was eventually convicted. When it was subsequently discovered what information Armani and Belge had documented and then kept secret, there was so much outrage in the community that they themselves were brought up before the State Bar Ethics Committee. Their defense was that they were simply acting in their client's best interest, which was their sole mandated role. Professor Guyers stopped at this point in the presentation and looked coyly at his expectant students. His lively brown eyes danced from one intent face to another.

"And what do you think," he proceeded after a moment, "was the outcome?"

A bunch of voices said various things overlapping each other. . . . "Illegal . . . disbarment . . . they ought to be fired. . . ."

He smiled. "Wrong. The committee found for the attorneys. Their decision was that it was not the lawyers' legal obligation to aid the state in separate and totally different murder investigations. In fact, in the interest of effective judicial administration, it was their obligation to adhere to the strict rule of confidentiality. Their exact language was, and I quote," he bent down to a little laptop computer in front of him, tapped a few keys, and read, "The lawyer's failure to disclose his knowledge of the two unrelated homicides was not improper, assuming that the information came to the lawyer during the course of his employment. Furthermore, the requirements of Canon Four that 'a lawyer should preserve the confidences and secrets of a client,' and of EC 4-1 and DR 4-101(B), would have been violated if such disclosure had been made." He looked up from the screen to make sure everyone was following him, then continued. "Proper representation of a client calls for full disclosure by the client to his lawyer of all possibly relevant facts, even though such facts may reveal the client's commission of prior crimes. To encourage full disclosure, the client must be assured of confidentiality, a requirement embodied by law in the attorney-client privilege and broadly incorporated in Canon Four of the Code."

He turned off the computer and brought down its screen with a click. "What that means is that while it may have been morally reprehensible to keep those parents agonizing over their losses for the long period of time it took to finish the trial, under our system of justice, 'morally reprehensible' does not always add up to 'legally actionable.' One must be clear about this distinction." While his students grumbled at a low level over this apparent travesty, he smiled indulgently. "Any comments?" He looked around the room again, but no one spoke. He was about to continue when Margaret raised her hand in the air. He looked at her and nodded.

"I remember," she began, "that when my husband Oscar died, well, he was very sick for a few months before and had a lot of time to think about the arrangements, you know, about the funeral and all."

Professor Guyers leaned back in his chair and tilted his head down. He dropped the glasses an inch lower on his nose and peered over the rim at her. "Yes?" he said expectantly.

"Well, one of the things he decided he wanted was to be buried with a deck of cards, a handball, a pack of cigarettes, and," she hesitated, "Ruffles." She looked around at her costudents who were now looking interested but also confused. "Ruffles was our seventeen-year-old pet terrier who was also very sick and who the vet had suggested we put to sleep. I guess Oscar thought it might be nice to have a friend in the Great Beyond." She shrugged. "Anyway, when the time came, the funeral director had no problem with the deck of cards, the handball, or the pack of cigarettes, but Ruffles was another matter. He said there were laws against burying animals in the same casket with humans. So Oscar went to Mount

Ararrat and Ruffles went to Happy Valley Crematorium, or so the vet claimed.''

"Um, could you get to the point, Mrs. Binton," the teacher said. "I don't really see how . . .''

"It's just that there are laws about burying people, about what can be buried with someone, and where they can be buried. Oscar also would have loved to be buried in the sand under the card tables at Rockaway Beach Club but he knew that was hopeless.'' She looked for a moment across the table at her costudents. "What I'm getting at is surely there must have been some laws that those two guys," she looked down at the notes she had been taking, "Armani and Belge, were breaking simply by not notifying authorities that they'd found two bodies in a state park. Maybe there was a way to get them on those kind of unrelated charges without compromising their lawyer/client relationship.''

The woman with the dashiki laughed. "Who are you kidding, honey. Lawyers were probably white. You think any court is going to mess with them over something so childish as . . .'' she looked for the right word . . . "sanitation? Now if they was black lawyers, like Vernon Mason, they'd have his hide in jail so quick for something as minor as an unpaid parking ticket.''

Margaret felt herself getting red in the face. "This is not a racial issue,'' she said. "It is a problem of finding some way to punish an immoral but apparently legal action. Think of the poor parents.''

The black woman snorted. "Talk about the real world, honey.''

"I thought this was a class in legal ethics, not social injustice,'' Margaret said tightly. "Perhaps you signed up for the wrong course.'' She shook her head. Why did everyone have a chip on their shoulder these days?

"But social injustice leads to change in law.'' This came from one of the Russian taxi drivers in an accent as thick as good borscht. "Is this not true? Is this not America? Mrs.

Wiggins is right, this is a hair you are trying to split, Mrs. Binton."

The Chinese man added his two cents. "He should have buried them somewhere else but in a state park."

The Czech repairman said, "At least it wasn't Central Park."

Margaret leaned back and sighed. God, how she wanted a cigarette. Just a few puffs even. Of course, there was no smoking in the classroom, and even if there was, she had done very well that day. . . . up until class time. What a bunch of difficult people. Couldn't they concentrate on the central issue? She looked at her teacher, who was still peering over his glasses at his students, this time with a more amused expression. Finally, he raised his hand and the confusion of voices subsided.

"In fact," he began, "Mrs. Binton is on to something." He pushed the glasses back up his nose and patted his computer again. "While the ethics committee threw out the action, one of the lawyers was subsequently indicted for two health law misdemeanors, one of which imposed a duty to provide a decedent with a decent burial and the other of which required disclosure of a death occurring without medical attention. That's the good news. The bad news is that the indictment was dismissed by the intermediate appellate court. I suppose one could say that the greater moral principle was at least acknowledged. Thank you, Mrs. Binton, for your," he took a breath, "persistence and creativity. I'm also glad to know your husband shared some of my favorite vices. My particular choice is pinochle." He looked down at his watch. "Let's take our ten minute coffee break now. When we get back, I want to bring up the next case, *Nix versus Whiteside*, which is all about counsel's foreknowledge of intentional perjury." He pushed back from the table and stood up. The other people in the room relaxed; some stood, some just leaned back. Margaret quickly headed for the door.

She found the phone booth in the adjoining corridor and pulled out Adrian's number. Please let him be home, she prayed. Just this one time when I need him. It's either that or I smoke the rest of my pack right here and now before I go back in that room. She fumbled with the change in her large handbag until she found a quarter, then dialed her young partner. She waited impatiently through four rings and was about to hang up when she heard his voice.

"Hello," he said. She thought he sounded strange. Very nervous.

"Adrian, it's Margaret Binton, your Smoke Stoppers partner. I need help." She heard the unmistakable sounds of him inhaling deeply on a cigarette. "Sounds like you do too," she added.

There was silence on the line.

"What's wrong? Margaret asked. "Did I catch you at a bad time?"

"I . . . I don't know. Probably nothing. I'm just being a little paranoid. It's this project I'm doing." He took another drag and slowly exhaled into the phone. Just what she needed! "What's your problem?" he said. "Another crossword puzzle making you crazy?"

"I wish. No, it's this course I'm taking. Legal ethics. Everyone has their own agenda and what you young people call an attitude. You know what I mean?"

"Makes you want to smoke?"

"And how."

"Fight it."

"Like you. You know what I think, Adrian. Maybe one day I can smoke for the both of us, and the next day you take over. That way at least we'll cut down in half."

"Not if we smoke twice as many cigarettes. You know what I think . . ." Margaret heard a noise in the background. Adrian's voice took on a more nervous timbre. "Hold on a minute," he said. She heard the receiver drop onto a table, heard noises of him opening and closing a door, then silence, and then he was back.

"No, it was nothing," he said.

"What did you expect? You know, you're making me more nervous than when I called."

"What I'm expecting is probably a figment of my creative brain. You know us writers." He took another drag and Margaret longed for the smoke that she knew was coursing through his lungs. Damn, she thought, this wasn't working.

"How about you chew some gum," he said.

"Very creative. Why don't you?"

"You don't need to worry about me, Margaret, this is the last cigarette in my pack."

"Listen, Adrian, I've got to get back to my class. There's this long corridor, maybe fifty steps to the room. How's this sound? If I make it past the thirtieth step without lighting up, I'll wait until later. If not, I'll smoke one puff for every five steps I do make."

"If it was me I'd light up in the thirtieth stride. I'm sure you're just as devious. How about for every five steps you do make, you smoke one puff and throw one cigarette away. You know, like the stick and the carrot. If you make it past thirty you get to keep them all."

"You are creative after all, Adrian. I'll try it. Meanwhile, what are you going to do?"

"Maybe I'll just have to put some shekels together and go to the local bodega," he said with a nervous laugh. "But I'm fighting it. Good luck, Margaret. See you at the next meeting." She heard a click as the phone was hung up. She replaced her receiver and turned to face the long corridor. Here goes, she thought, and started counting.

Five minutes later the break was over and Professor Guyers began on *Nix v. Whiteside*. One crushed butt and five unsmoked cigarettes were in the wall ashtray by the classroom door. At this rate, Margaret figured, she'd have to stop smoking before her own supply of shekels ran out.

# 4

Adrian Lavin left the little grocery store on Columbus and pulled his raincoat closer together at the neck. It was getting colder out, and with the steady drizzle he had hesitated for over an hour after Margaret's call before going to buy another pack of cigarettes. It wasn't true that he couldn't write a word without a haze of smoke curling between his thoughts and the screen, but it certainly helped. Besides, this Smoke Stoppers thing was something he did almost as a concession to the antismoking climate sweeping the country in general, and his friends in particular. He actually liked smoking, liked the whole damn process right from the moment when he laid his money on the counter and was given a new, elegantly geometrical package, wrapped in cool cellophane. As far as he was concerned, the promise in that pack delivered more consistently than even the Entenmann's chocolate chip cookies he treated himself to once a week. He was trying to be a socially conscious, politically correct post-yuppie, but this particular struggle was one he felt slipping away from him.

He opened the package, lit another cigarette, and started walking back up the block towards his building. As he walked, he looked at his block: The brownstones close to Columbus with their poorer, rent-controlled tenants, the townhouses midblock with their gentrified upwardly mobile middle class, and finally, straddling the corner on Central Park West, the two large prewar co-op apartment towers with their established bankers and lawyers. A block like many others on the Upper West Side that mixed social strata, ethnic and religious diversity, and levels of wealth as efficiently as if everything had been put into a blender. Somehow, through it all, everyone managed to coexist. Except this evening there was something menacing about the block that Adrian could almost feel. At 9:45 the street was deserted. The rain was keeping everyone indoors or in taxicabs up on the avenues. But it wasn't just the emptiness. He'd walked this street at 3:00 A.M. and felt more secure. It was something else, something that had been said to him more than six hours earlier. The threat . . .

Adrian lived in the ground-floor apartment of one of the townhouses midblock. It had been sheer luck that had gotten him the space three years earlier, a matter, for once in his life, of perfect timing. He happened to be walking by at the same time the landlord was taping the FOR RENT sign in the window. Of course the space was tiny, probably less than four hundred square feet, but it had a private bathroom, a functioning kitchen, and a window on a back garden. Adrian had been living at the YMCA downtown and to his mind this was a quantum leap upward. His friends had questioned the safety of a ground-floor apartment, but the windows were barred and the quick access was one of the things Adrian liked. From street to apartment in five seconds.

Now he wished he were inside. He had another thirty yards to walk, then a three-step drop down into a little fenced-in patio to the side of the stoop in front of his door. He took a long drag on the cigarette and looked behind him. Why was he so nervous? There was no one on the block behind him, no one in front of him. . . . Still, he didn't slow his pace. This city is finally getting to me, he thought.

He turned into his little entranceway and reached into his pocket for his keys. There was the slightest sound of rustling fabric, but it did not come from him. It came from the shadows under the stoop four feet away. He started to look up, but not quickly enough to see the blade of the six-inch knife as it drove from out of the darkness into his chest. Adrian only had time to utter a surprised "unh" before he felt something so fascinatingly wrong in his body, so horrifyingly altered, that he dropped to the pavement without another sound. He was just able to look down at the handle of the knife protruding from his chest and realize the enormity of what had happened before the tide of blackness overcame him. He died with the cigarette still burning between his lips and his hand clutching the ring of keys in his pocket.

# 5

Margaret found out about the death the same way thousands of other New Yorkers did, through her morning newspaper. But Adrian's death had happened so late in the evening, that it had only made it into Section B, page six, as a one-inch side box. Margaret had passed over the little article on her way to the crossword before she realized that this Adrian Lavin who had been found dead, presumedly from a street mugging, might be her young friend. It took a long moment to register, even after she brought all the details together, until she finally got up, and went to rummage in her desk drawer. The paper with the names of the Smoke Stopper students was wedged inside one of their brochures. Nervously, she traced down the list until her finger came to rest on Adrian's name and address, the same as in the article.

She felt light-headed and frighteningly short of breath. Certainly from the scant description in the paper, she must have been one of the last people to have spoken to him. He had been killed at 10:00 P.M., just over an hour and a half after their phone conversation. Still clutching the Smoke Stoppers brochure, she went back to her easy chair and slowly sank down. She ran through that phone call again, remembering his suggestions about her throwing one cigarette away for every puff she took. But what she remembered even more vividly was how nervous he was, the little noises he went to check on.

She sat in thought for another five minutes, and at the end of that time she had made up her mind. It took her only fifteen minutes to get ready, putting on her no-nonsense blue gabardine dress, thick-soled Dr. Scholl's knockoffs, and maroon woolen beret to cover the hastily arranged hair bun. Lieutenant Morley would be in. She tried calculating how long it had been since her last delivery of homemade cookies. Three weeks, a month? Certainly not too long for him to still be civilized to her. It was always good, she realized, to start on the right foot. Especially with Morley, who could, depending on the state of his workload, turn from innocent charmer into a fire-breathing dragon. She had experienced first-hand with her friend Morley the true meaning of the word "volatile." At moments like that, the only thing she had going for her were the cookies and the fact that she had helped him on a few recent police matters; precious little when it came to keeping conversations reasonably polite. But, she did have some important information, and if she caught him in the right mood . . . She slammed the door hard behind her and headed for the elevator. Now if only she could avoid her friends on the way. The last thing she wanted was to be delayed by idle chitchat.

The 81st Precinct was on the block between Columbus and Amsterdam on Eighty-second Street. It was a postwar building of such crushing nondescription as to wonder if an architect or aluminum-siding salesman had been hired as chief designer. The nicest thing you could say about it was that the front door was wide enough to admit a cop escorting a crackhead and still have enough room to pass the other way. Since there appeared to be a fairly steady stream of such traffic, this was no idle measurement. Margaret passed into the inner hallway and announced her intentions to Sergeant Kivlehan, the desk officer.

"Jesus Christ, Margaret," he said. "You have to see him *now*? They just pulled off a bust of a crackhouse over on West Ninetieth."

"So I noticed." She straightened her back to add another half inch to her five-foot-two-inch stature. "It's about the Lavin murder. I knew him, I . . . spoke to him just before he was killed."

Kivlehan looked carefully at her for a moment and slowly shook his head. "Damned, Margaret, if you don't have a knack for choosing some funny friends now. Sure you must be the luckiest lady in the precinct." He leaned back. "You knew him, did you say?"

She nodded.

"Well then, I guess you should see Morley." He motioned her down a hallway and picked up the phone on his desk. By the time Margaret had arrived in front of Morley's door, it was open and the good lieutenant himself was holding the knob. Now, what was this? Margaret wondered. He had a smile on his face?

"Molasses lace today, I hope," he said. "The almond butter killed my cholesterol count."

Margaret looked at his profile in the doorway and passed through. "One would think the molasses cookies would kill your clothing allowance. You up over two hundred again?"

"That's for me to know and my doctor to find out. You don't qualify." He followed her in and pulled out a chair for her. He really was feeling expansive. He had grabbed the comfortable Naugahyde one, not the hard wooden side chair.

Margaret sat down and looked over the desk in front of her. There were stacks of paper, an ashtray, empty coffee cups, and assorted objects that Morley had picked up over the years: a pair of brass knuckles he used as a paperweight, a few empty cartridges in a ceramic box, a jar of stale jelly beans. . . .

"I noticed you were busy this morning," Margaret said.

Morley threw up his hands. "Druggies. They're all over the place," he said disgustedly. "And they're getting cuter by the day." He came and sat down, shuffled some papers on his desk, then reached under one of them and lifted something up. It was a green plastic vial four inches long with a spike on the bottom and a rubber stopper with a small hole in it on the top.

"Someone giving you roses, Sam? How thoughtful."

"Very good, Margaret. I'm impressed." He looked at her steadily. "You're probably the only other person in this building who knows what those things are. I had to ask someone downtown."

"If you do volunteer work in the hospital," Margaret said, "you come across a lot of gift roses. Most of the expensive ones come with those contraptions on the stems to keep them fresh. They hold water and the spike gets stuck in green Styrofoam. Personally, I prefer vases myself."

"Yeah, well, these are not for roses," Morley continued. "It's some new method of merchandising cocaine. Holds up to five grams neatly, but the interesting part is the little spike. Dealer buries these into the ground upside down any place there's dirt with just the end of the spike showing. Never has to have possession of the material. Limits his liability, although there are ways for us around it.

We just started finding these things, probably from one dealer. The problem is, he's not too bright. Instead of cutting his stuff with mannite, he's cutting it with strychnine, which is usually used in cutting heroin. Unfortunately people ingest greater volumes of cocaine than of heroin, so they are getting greater quantities of the strychnine. In the last two months we've already had five wind up in the hospital emergency ward with these things in their pocket. This little bust we just had . . ." he motioned outside to the flow of people past his door, "was to try and get some leads." He leaned back in his chair and smiled at the older woman in front of him. "That's why all the activity. But you didn't come for a lecture on the new mechanics of drug dealing. Kivlehan said something about Lavin?"

Margaret nodded. "Yes, we were in Smoke Stoppers together." She pulled out a pack of cigarettes and lit one up, then unceremoniously tossed the match over a stack of papers, and the little rose stem moistener to land in the ashtray on the lieutenant's desk. The expression on his face turned into a wry grin.

"You flunk out?"

"Just temporarily." She wrote the cigarette down in her little journal, wrapped it up in the rubber band, and put the package back in her large handbag. "He was my partner, the person I was supposed to call when things got too difficult. I spoke to him about eight-thirty last night."

"Yeah, well . . ." Morley scratched his head. "He was killed about an hour and a half later, right in front of his door. The mugger got his wallet. He still had his keys and a new pack of cigarettes, so we checked with the local all-night grocery. The clerk remembered him coming in and paying for the butts from his wallet. He was a regular there and the clerk knew him well."

"Sam, he wasn't mugged," Margaret said softly. "When I spoke to him he was scared of something, really jumpy."

Morley took a deep breath. "Margaret, damn if you don't always see something arch in even the most mundane mugging. I hate to say this, but the same kind of thing happens a dozen times a week in New York. We don't get so many in this precinct, but we're unusual. Lavin must have had a bunch of bills in his wallet that someone noticed in the store; they followed him the half-block back and jumped him in the little alcove. Picture perfect."

"The knife wound was from the back?"

Morley hesitated. "No, from in front. He must have asked him for his money first and Lavin refused."

27

"It's too easy, Sam. It just doesn't feel right. Was there anything else that was unusual?"

Morley shook his head. "Like I said, a dozen a week." He leaned forward and pulled a manila envelope from his desk. He looked up at her speculatively. "You want to see the initial Polaroids?"

"Just one." She reached out and Morley handed a picture across the desk.

"Is that him?" the lieutenant asked.

She nodded but continued to study the picture. After a moment she put it down.

"You get many muggings where the victim's hand is still in his pocket?"

Morley shifted in his seat and looked down at another one of the black-and-whites he had in his lap. "So?"

"Some one follows him home, confronts him for money, and Adrian has enough time to turn around but not enough to take his hand out of his pocket?" She sounded skeptical. "Don't you find that peculiar?"

"Margaret, when it comes to murder, peculiar is where it's at. We responded once to a stabbing and found the victim at his kitchen table eating some pork. Punctured kidney, massive internal hemorrhaging, and he's calmly feeding his face. He had fried up some chops before the argument and he was damned if he was going to let them go to waste. Died about twenty minutes later when they were bringing him down to the ambulance. Peculiar, sure, but we get it all the time."

"But in this case, significant." Margaret took another puff on her cigarette and stabbed it out in Morley's ashtray. "Because it indicates that he didn't have time to do anything. I don't think someone followed him, Sam, I think someone was waiting for him. That's a big difference." She was silent for a few moments. Finally she asked, "I don't suppose there were any witnesses?"

"Maybe yes, maybe no."

"What's that supposed to mean?" she said frowning. "They were wearing dark sunglasses?"

"Very funny. No, we got a report from a Mrs. Evarts who was looking out at the rain from five stories up. She didn't hear anything, or actually see the murder, but she saw someone running down the street. She thinks he may have come from Lavin's building since she hadn't seen him running further up the block."

"A lot of people run in the rain."

"That's what I told her, but she claimed that there was something funny about this man. He ran kind of looking behind him now and then."

"A man?" Margaret repeated. "Anything else?"

Morley looked at his notes. "Yeah, here it is, short, dark hair, little mustache, sneakers, stocky . . ."

Margaret sighed. "Half the men in New York."

A little smile was playing across Morley's face. It was the kind of look he saved up for his lectures on community action programs. Patient, sincere, condescending. He reached out for the photo and Margaret handed it back.

"So, maybe someone was waiting," he said finally. "His wallet's still missing. Could be they saw him leave, figure he's only going out to the store and wait for him to come back."

She snorted. "The trouble with you cops is that sometimes you've seen far too much to be really creative. Ever notice how it's the beginners with the slowest questions and the experts with the quickest answers? I'd like to see it the other way around once. I tell you Adrian was scared of something an hour before he was murdered and that's a coincidence that can't be overlooked. Maybe you can, but I can't."

"What's that supposed to mean?" Morley asked, his awkward smile quickly fading from his face.

Margaret stood up and adjusted the little hat on the top of her head. "It means that I think you should stop wasting the taxpayer's money halfheartedly looking for a mugger that doesn't exist. Look for the real murderer, someone who had threatened him." She walked to the door and turned the knob. "And if you don't, I will."

"Margaret, don't you have anything better to do with your time? Volunteer work at a hospital or something? Maybe making cookies for the homeless? Something reasonable."

"You know, Sam, just once in your life you should try listening. It may be an art, but it's one that even a moose like you can learn. Condescension suits you about as well as hair on an egg." She walked through the door and left Morley staring after her. The hair comment had been calculated to let Morley know just how angry she was. Morley's head was as slick as a robin's egg and his ego just as sensitive. Margaret rarely sank to such low blows and it gave Lieutenant Morley pause. But pause to a lieutenant with a pen full of crackheads to process was a luxury he couldn't prolong. Five minutes after Margaret had left, Morley was deep into the papers on his desk, had put an assistant DA on hold, and was arranging transportation for ten assorted felons down to Centre Street.

Morley knew the Lavin murder was going to be taken over by Tony Renzuli in Homicide anyway, so he figured he was out of it. If Margaret wanted to get hot and bothered about it, she could damn well do it with someone else. He put the phone down and ran a hand over his bald head. "Ingrate," he said, and reached for the phone, remembering the DA on hold. But before switching him back on he hesitated just long enough to remember some of the other times Margaret had an idea contrary to his. Instead of picking up with the young DA, he pushed another of his outside lines and dialed a number. When a voice came on he said gruffly into the phone, "Get me Renzuli over in Homicide."

# 6

The Florence E. Bliss Senior Citizens Center was alive with activity when Margaret arrived in the middle of the morning, the kind of activity that appeared to have been shot at 48 frames per second. Slow motion was invented by filmmakers, but in real life it was practiced by casts of people with bursitis, arthritis, sciatica, rheumatism, and a dozen other ailments. The six card tables were being used, mostly for gin and Scrabble, the coffee table and snack area were well attended, and the television lounge had only two free chairs. There were only a few people on their feet, changing commitments from one two-hour activity to another. But lack of movement did not mean in any way lack of communication. If anything, all the people in the Center felt obliged to make up for their sedentary activities by talking incessantly about anything and everything that passed in front of them. Margaret had heard conversations lasting for over a half hour on the subject of light pulls and others equally as long on the difference between 68 and 69 degrees Fahrenheit. And to be truthful, Margaret knew that she had participated in some of those conversations herself.

The Center itself looked clean and pleasant, with bright fluorescent lights and shiny linoleum floors, but the furniture was a hodgepodge of styles and materials that could only be called "thrift shop antique." Used and scarred aluminum chairs and tables were scattered amidst divans and sofas that looked as worn as a seat in an Eighth Avenue porn movie. The few items of art on the walls had been donated by two local merchants, a plumbing-supply store and a tourist office. Mad Ludwig's castle, the Coliseum, and the Eiffel Tower vied for wall space with calendars showing pipe stems and fittings from the Rigid Company. But no one there noticed the lack of a cohesive design theme in their surroundings. What they noticed immediately was snow on the television or dregs in their coffee. Everything else was just landscape to be glided through carefully and slowly. In this way, the world outside was, at least temporarily, kept at bay. Except that Margaret was a master at bringing that world inside, which was why she was both so frightening and interesting to her friends. Interesting just as long as they could remain bystanders and let her do all the flitting. Which was, of course, not at all what Margaret had in mind this day.

"Berdie," she was now saying, "you have to help me with this. I can't do it alone."

Berdie Mangione raised her thin, bird-like face and stared in disbelief at her friend. They had been through a lot of things in the forty years they'd known each other, but this was one of the most ridiculous. Even crazier than when they picketed the condo, crazy enough this time to land them in jail. She puffed herself out to her full five-foot-one inches, took a deep breath and said simply, "No."

"But you have to," Margaret said. "I need a lookout."

"No," Berdie repeated. "It's too dangerous. Just because you know how to get into his apartment doesn't give you permission to enter." She paused for a moment and squinted at her friend. "How'd you get a key, anyway?"

"I don't have it yet. Adrian once told me that he kept one at the dry cleaners' for some maid that came now and then. When things got too piled up. It just depends on how long a memory the cleaner has."

"You're going to pretend you're a maid?" Berdie asked in disbelief.

"It's worth a try. I'd like to get a look at his things, especially what he was working on." She lowered her voice and leaned closer to her friend, almost spilling the coffee cup on the table in front of her. "I don't think the police are staking out the apartment since he was killed outside, but we could walk by first and check it out."

Berdie raised an eyebrow. "Then what?" she asked.

"Then I get the key and you wait outside while I go in. All you have to do is sit on the stoop reading and if a policeman comes down the block just tap on the window."

Berdie shifted on her seat. "I stay outside, right?"

Margaret smiled innocently. "That's right."

"And that's only if you get the key?"

"Uh huh."

Berdie thought for a long moment, looking around her at the quiet surroundings. Finally she shrugged. "Well okay, but you can only stay for a few minutes inside. I'd get palpitations if you were in there for very long."

Margaret patted her knee. "But of course. I don't want to spend a lot of time inside his apartment either. Thanks, dear, I knew you'd want to help." She finished off her coffee and sat back. The two women were silent for a minute as Margaret reached in her bag for a Kleenex.

"You know, Margaret, my Tony had you pegged right from the start." Berdie said. "Poor man had a weak heart, but a good head. He told me you had more spunk than a roomful of teamsters. That it was just Oscar holding you back."

Margaret smiled wistfully. "Oscar was a bit conservative, I'll admit, wasn't he? But then again," she blew her nose, "I think I liked that. He could be real stubborn when he got behind a 'no.' Almost as stubborn as I was behind a 'yes.'

33

I think it made for a good balance. Certainly made for a lively marriage.''

"But did he ever get his way, I mean on the big things? I don't suppose that was likely with you.''

There was another silence, this time for a longer moment. Margaret put the tissue back in her bag and snapped it shut.

"One issue,'' she said sadly. "He didn't want children. I was working then and I let it get away from me. You know Oscar and I got married late and I guess I just let it slide. By the time I knew I wanted them, we were into a comfortable routine, we were in our forties, and Oscar just said no. It was almost as though he was saving up a little something from each argument he had lost, and all that anger and determination went into the argument about kids. I'd never seen him so determined.'' She sighed. "It came down to a matter of either no children or divorce, and I knew he was being deadly serious. So I made a decision, the hardest one I think I've ever made.'' She pushed back from the table and brushed the crumbs off her lap. "And I've been regretting it ever since.'' She smiled thinly. "So what can I tell you, one huge loss and a lot of little successes. That's life, I guess.''

"Not mine,'' Berdie said. "Tony and me never argued because nothing would ever get that far. All he had to do was raise his voice and I gave in.'' She shrugged. "Silly, huh, living a life like that, but at the time it seemed the easiest thing to do.'' Berdie stood up and came over to help Margaret. "Now listen to us nattering away like two old hens. Before you know it we'll be like the rest of these old geezers, living their lives in the past.''

"God forbid,'' Margaret said standing up. "No percentage in that.'' She grabbed hold of Berdie's hand and the two of them trotted out of the Center.

34

# 7

The two women slowly walked down the block from Central Park West to Columbus Avenue. A nasty damp fog had settled over the city and sent a chill up Berdie's thin frame. Margaret pulled her overcoat closer around her neck. As they walked they were chatting animatedly and looked as though they were in their own little world. As they approached the small brownstone where the killing had occurred the day before, Margaret angled ever so slightly towards the building line. It was lunchtime, but few people were on the block due to the weather. Margaret noticed a yellow piece of plastic tape roping off the little alcove where Adrian had lost his life, but there was not a single policeman in sight. The crime-scene unit had already left, after doing what they could in the tiny concrete space. Margaret looked over into the ground-floor window, but no lights were on and the place looked deserted. Now for the key, she thought, and the two women continued on down the block. When they hit Columbus they turned left and stopped.

"Which cleaner is it?" Berdie asked. She indicated the two on the opposite sides of the street.

"Well if it was me, I'd patronize the closest one. No one wants to walk one step further than they have to carrying dirty clothing. I'll bet Adrian was the same. You wait here. I'll be back in a minute. The murder happened last night. I hope they haven't put two and two together." Berdie waited by one of the parking meters and watched as Margaret entered the store.

"Yeah?" the young Puerto Rican man said as Margaret stopped in front of the counter.

"Oh, hello," she said brightly. "I'm Belle Danziger, Mr. Lavin's maid. He told me last week that I could pick up the key to his apartment here."

The young man looked her over once and leaned closer. He had a bundle of dirty shirts in his arm that he had been trying to stuff into a large bag.

"Who?"

"Lavin," she repeated. "Fifty-four West Ninetieth." She looked at her watch. "Did I get the right cleaner? I'm already a half-hour late."

"Just a minute," the man said. He struggled for another few seconds and managed to stuff the shirts into the bag. In the process, one of the buttons snagged on the edge and tore a little rip in a pocket.

"Some people are slobs, hey?" he muttered. "Two months' worth of shirts here. Ones on the bottom are ready for a decent burial. Lavin, huh? I'll see what they got. I don't usually work the front but Tony went out to the bank." He reached under the counter and pulled up a metal file box. On the top, marked in crayon was the word "keys." When he opened it Margaret caught a glimpse of at least a dozen keys with little tags attached. As the man looked through them, Margaret shifted uneasily from foot to foot.

"I guess Mr. Lavin's one of your busy young lawyers or accountants who never make it home before midnight," he said.

"Something like that," Margaret said noncommittally. "We get a lot of them yuppies. They all got people coming to clean or deliver stuff that they don't want to give keys to. Mostly the people in the brownstones. I guess Tony does this as a favor. Yeah, here it is." He lifted out a ring with two keys on it and turned the tag over. " 'Lavin's maid,' it says here. I guess that means you." He looked at her expectant seventy-two-year-old face again, then handed it across the counter. "Just bring it back by eight." He smiled, hefted the sack of shirts and tossed them medicine ball-like into a bin towards the back of the store. "Phew. Good riddance," he added after the bag.

Margaret turned back out of the door. As she hit the pavement she let out a little sigh and stuffed the key into her handbag. There certainly were some advantages to looking nonthreatening, she thought. She found Berdie where she had left her and the two of them walked back up the block.

"Any problems?" Berdie asked.

"Don't ever go there if you want your blouses cleaned," Margaret said.

"No, I mean with the key. He didn't know Adrian had just been murdered?"

Margaret shook her head. "No, or if he did he didn't pick up on the name. But tomorrow by this time, everyone on the block will know. Don't be so nervous, Berdie." She looked at her out of the corner of her eye. "You got a book with you?"

Berdie nodded and lifted one out of a shopping bag she was carrying. It was a little torn and Margaret recognized the stamp of the Florence E. Bliss library on its back.

"Good, just so you don't look too conspicuous."

"Oh no," Berdie said sarcastically, "I won't look too conspicuous sitting in the middle of a roped-off murder scene reading some book I just grabbed called . . . what is it? *Financial Strategies for the Eighties.*"

"A little outdated, wouldn't you say?"

"Never mind, here we are. Make it snappy." She looked

around again at the empty block and ducked under the tape. "I'll wait here."

Margaret followed and opened the front door with one of the keys. Inside, a little hallway lit with a single low-wattage bulb led to two doors. Margaret tried the one in back and found herself facing a dim room with a boiler and water heaters and old suitcases and skis. She backed out and tried the other door but that was locked. The second key opened the door and she quietly entered Adrian's apartment.

A misty, gray light filtered in through the front window, but it was enough to let her see around the small studio. The single room was furnished sparely with a desk, a dining table next to it, a bed, an old easy chair, a wall of bookcases made out of wooden planks and bricks, and a single bureau. Things seemed to be arranged without a sense of function. The dining table was not near the small kitchen, the bureau was on the other side of the room from the bed, and the easy chair was nowhere near the bookcases. It looked rather like the movers had just finished delivering and the tenant had yet to put a hand to arranging things. But Adrian was consistent. Margaret saw that even the desk top had papers spilling every which way, including onto the dining table between dirty dishes. A small laptop computer was in the center of all the mess on the desk, looking somewhat out of place in its neat white plastic case. Books were on the floor in stacks where they couldn't fit into the stuffed bookcase, and dirty clothes and used towels were spilling out of a laundry bag under the bed. It was no wonder Adrian needed a cleaning lady. Margaret moved over into the tiny kitchen and shook her head. Maybe a family of cleaners, by the look of things. More dirty dishes, opened and spilled cereal boxes, stuffed garbage can. Her quick glance told her that there was nothing for her there and she turned back into the squarish room. She could see Berdie's silhouette through the curtained window sitting on the windowsill. So, she'd try to be quick, but there was a mountain of stuff and she had no idea what she was looking for.

She went over and sat down at the desk chair. All the papers looked like notes that should have been on index cards but had been ripped out of some journal. Many had been bundled together with paper clips, others were lying singly exposed. Over most of them was a red check mark as though they had been dealt with in some way. In total there must have been a grocery box full of them, too many to even try to make sense of now. She quickly read through a few, then bent to open the two desk drawers in front of her. More of the same disorganization. Pens and paper clips, Band-Aids and matches were tossed together into one box, new envelopes were mixed in with old forgotten laundry tickets and movie stubs. This disorder was frightening.

She opened the drawer further and saw a folder with papers inside. Finally some order. She opened it and found several letters from Divinity Publishing Company, including something that looked like a contract.

"Now we're getting somewhere," Margaret breathed, and sat back to read through the correspondence.

Berdie wasn't really following the discussion of leveraged buyouts so much as using the book as a shield to hide her darting eyes. Every car that came down the block was inspected to see if it contained one of New York's Finest who, she was convinced, once spotting her sitting there, would immediately send her to jail for twenty years. Maybe with a smart lawyer she could plea-bargain it down to ten years, but that didn't make her feel any less vigilant. Margaret had been inside now over a half hour and Berdie was nearly faint from nervous tension. And she said she'd be quick!

Once a police car did drive down the block, but it went so quickly that by the time she thought of knocking on the window it had already passed. There was still not too much foot traffic for such a pretty block, but cars kept pushing through. One of them—a taxicab—passed her and pulled over about fifty feet to her right. She kept watching, waiting idly for the door to open, but nothing happened. Finally the cab driver got out and angrily pulled on the passenger door. Berdie couldn't hear everything that was said, but the gist of the argument was plain. The rider didn't have the fare and the cab driver was kicking him out. . . . most likely after they had gotten to the rider's destination. A typical New York method of transportation, but Berdie kept her eyes on the fracas nonetheless. With her attention drawn away, she didn't notice the tall woman and the short man, both in dark raincoats, as they walked down the block from her left. She didn't notice them stop, stare at her, then angle in towards the stoop. She came to, however, when they lifted the tape and walked up to her.

"I can see you know how to read," the woman said, pointing at the book. "Too bad you can't follow directions. The tape says this is a crime scene. You gotta go." She motioned with her head out onto the sidewalk.

Berdie felt her face turning red, but managed to keep her voice from sounding shaky.

"What's the problem, lady? I can't sit down to rest my feet here? You the landlord or something?"

The woman flashed a badge and motioned again. "Come on, find some place else to rest.

"Police?" Berdie raised her voice. "Yes ma'am, whynt'-cha say that in the first place." She put her hands on the windowsill to raise herself, and as she did her two elbows banged against the glass. She stood up, closed the book, and put it in her shopping bag. "Okay, I'm going." Berdie said.

"Hold it. You got a name?" the short man asked.

"Doesn't everybody?" she answered and turned toward the two steps up onto the street. She knew she'd be proud of that one for at least a month, but right now she was too angry at herself to care. And nervous. The short cop moved to stand in her way, but the woman he was with motioned him away.

"Let her go, Sonny. We got other things to do. Come on, you got the key?" Berdie moved away quickly, cursing her stupidity. How had she allowed them to sneak up on her? Damn! Now what? She felt her breaths coming on shorter and shorter as she walked, and she had to sit down on one of the benches that lined the park. She had the same sense of doom the time Tony had been taken to the hospital that last time, the same knowledge that life would be different. God knows where they'll send Margaret, she thought. I wonder if they have special prisons for people on Social Security. Maybe they'll be able to trace me? She thought a thousand troubled thoughts, but mostly she sat on her bench, riveted with fear. She stayed like that for over an hour, then got up and walked home. There was nothing to do but wait.

The two police officers opened the door to Adrian's apartment and flipped on the light switch. This was the second time they'd been inside the apartment, but the first time had been mostly to find out names and addresses of people to notify. Lavin had been mugged outside his door, so there was no real reason to toss the place for clues or prints. But Morley over in the 81st had gotten to their boss in Homicide, and Lieutenant Renzuli had pushed them back out the door. These things happen. The two officers knew that favors are owed and it's a smart department head who keeps his precinct commanders cooperative. Besides, it wasn't any skin off Tony Renzuli. He wasn't the one who had to spend an hour searching the apartment. No, that was going to be the special privilege of Sergeants Edwards and Green, affectionately known by their peers as Scratch and Sniff. Sonny Edwards was Scratch since he looked like he shaved only every other day, and had a voice to match. Laura Green was Sniff, every cop's wife's nightmare, a thirty-two-year-old Sigourney Weaver look-alike with clear eyes, perfect posture, and a cloud of sensuality that swirled around her like a Nova Scotia fog. But she was as straight as Carrie Nation.

The two of them made an amusing team, but one not without success. They had been shifted to Renzuli in Homicide over two years earlier and hadn't let too many cases stay open on their desks. They worked effectively together, sometimes pushing the good cop/bad cop routine past its natural

41

limits. Today, however, they had no one to interrogate, just a one-room apartment to scan, which they put down to local stroking. Scratch and Sniff hated it, and they were in a foul mood as they started their search.

"What a goddamn mess this place is," Edwards said. He looked around at all the flat surfaces covered with papers and shook his head. "What exactly are we looking for?"

"Names. We already got his address book, but there could be other stuff. Letters, notes . . ." She moved over to the closet and put her hand on the knob. "Maybe he's got something in one of his pockets. Recent acquaintances, places he's been." She turned the knob and threw the door open. Adrian's closet was not quite as messy as his room and she was able to search the clothes methodically. As she found things, she examined them and then put them back. After a few minutes she closed the door. "Nothing," she said. She eyed the room professionally, then went over to the bed. "Sometimes the interesting stuff they hide under here." She got down on her hands and knees and peered underneath. "Like dust balls." She shook her head and stood up.

"Morley told Renzuli he got a tip that someone might have threatened him." Edwards was sitting at the desk, going through some of the notes. "You can't tell it from this. It's just a bunch of quotes, little notes . . . no names or nothing. Kind of like field notes."

Green came over and looked over his shoulder. "Yeah, he was a free-lance writer. Maybe it was for a magazine article. What are those letters on top of each note? E, C, H, P . . ."

Edwards shrugged. "Some kind of index system. Think we should take them?" He sounded like the last thing he wanted to do was collect a ton of paper scraps.

Green thought about that for a moment. "Without names? It's not going to help us much. Keep looking for something with a name. We can always come back to get those later. I'm going to look in the kitchen." She moved away and spent some time rummaging in the cabinets and broom closet. When she was finished she went into the bathroom and looked through the medicine cabinet. Twenty minutes later she was back, satisfied that nothing had escaped her search. "Find anything?"

"Only this," Edwards said. "Some letters. Checkbook. Rent stubs. That's about it. I mean besides the usual junk like Safeway coupons and matchbooks." He grinned. "I didn't look inside all the covers though."

"Maybe Renzuli would like to do that himself. You find out what he was working on?" He shook his head. She took another general sweep of the room and motioned to her partner. "Come on, let's go. There's nothing here. Let's go upstairs and try the neighbors. Then if Renzuli still isn't satisfied we can start in on the address book." Edwards stood up and followed his partner out, snapping off the light before slamming the door behind him.

Margaret breathed a sigh of relief when she heard the door upstairs slam. She was slumped down behind the hot water boiler and had a pair of skis pressing into her side. On her lap were the small computer and the folder of letters from Divinity Publishing. She waited another ten minutes, then unbent her body and stood up. Oh, the stiffness! She waited a moment until her muscles stopped screaming at her. The basement space was totally dark except for a thin crack of light that came in under the door. She slowly headed in that direction, and after a minute found the doorknob. There were no other sounds from the basement, so she cautiously made her exit into the hallway, and, a minute later, repeated the process to get outside.

She had just crept under the yellow crime scene tape and started walking stiffly back towards the cleaners when the top door of the stoop opened and the two police officers emerged. Green was noting something on a pad of paper. They didn't notice Margaret a half-dozen yards ahead of them carrying the little computer and folder of letters. They walked behind her until they reached their car, then got in and drove off. Margaret kept walking, dropped the keys back off at the dry

43

cleaners and headed downtown. She'd call Berdie right away, then a nice cup of tea, she thought. The two of them could go through the letters, and maybe if they were real lucky, they could figure out the computer. If not, she'd have to find someone who could. There was no doubt that the information she wanted was lurking somewhere in the thin little machine. But how to get it?

# 8

Y ou were *where?*" Berdie nearly screamed when she walked in Margaret's door. "My God, you had me scared half to death. I was sure you were going to get ten years."

"No, only pulled tendons and strained back muscles. Ever try to sit Indian style with a hunk of metal poking into your side, bent over double and hardly breathing?" She closed the door behind her friend and led her over to where the hot pot of tea with its cozy sat in the middle of the dining table. "I definitely do not recommend it for anyone over the age of twenty-eight." She poured the liquid into two waiting cups. "But now, dear, you could have given me a few moments more warning. It was a good thing I saw everyone's shadow and got nervous before you tapped on the window. Were they plainclothes?"

Berdie nodded.

"I figured," Margaret said. "Here, have some tea. You look exhausted. Were you worrying about me?" she asked innocently.

Berdie sat down, took a swallow, then another, then shook her head. "Margaret, if you ever scare me like that again, you can get yourself a new friend. I nearly died when those cops went in the apartment." She took another swallow and set the cup back down. A little grin crossed her face. "I stiffed them good, though. They wanted to know who I was but they didn't get a thing. I just kept walking away."

"Good for you," Margaret said. She took a sip of tea herself and settled down next to her friend.

"So did you find anything?" Berdie asked.

"I think so. He had a folder of letters from a Divinity Publishing Company and a contract for a book called *A St. Martin's Centennial.* Then there were all these notes strewn about with quotes and little bits of information about different people. All lettered in some sort of code. No names. But I couldn't find anything to decipher who was who." She took another sip of tea and continued. "Unless it's in here." She lifted from the floor the thin computer and put it on the table between them. "This was Adrian's. But I have no idea how to operate it. If I had to make a guess, I'd say he put everything in here after taking his field notes outside. They all seem to have been checked off like they were entered somewhere." She looked over at her friend. "By any chance do you know how to operate one of these things?"

"Margaret, you must be kidding. The only machine I know how to use is a Water Pik and even then I sometimes squirt myself in the face."

Margaret frowned. "How about Sid or any of the others?"

Berdie shook her head. "No way, dear. We would have heard. Our generation is still too fascinated by air travel to notice what's happening with silicon chips."

"Surely we can find someone who knows about them." She opened the top of the case and flipped up the hinged screen. "How hard can it be?" She reached behind and turned a switch and the screen danced with light. Berdie pushed back a good six inches from the table.

"Be careful dear, you're going to blow us up."

"Nonsense, it's just a matter of knowing what buttons to push. Maybe this one here. . . ." She pushed something and the computer beeped.

"Nope," Berdie said and leaned closer. "Maybe this one." She moved her hand closer and pressed the button marked CTRL. Another beep. Slowly, one by one, they pressed each button and were rewarded by 83 separate beeps. The screen remained a flat sheet of light. Margaret sighed.

"Maybe some combination," she said.

"Are you kidding? We could be here all night."

"You're right," Margaret said. "We need some help." She stood up and walked back and forth in front of the little television that was in a corner of the room. Finally she stopped. "And I know just who to ask. Professor Guyers, my teacher at NYU. He has a machine just like this one. I see him tomorrow evening anyway, after my meeting with Barbara Fleischer."

Berdie frowned. "I thought I knew all of your friends. Who's Barbara Fleischer?"

"I just spoke to her for the first time on the phone after I called you. She was Adrian's editor at Divinity Publishing, the woman who signed all the letters. She was very upset about Adrian's death, and willing to talk to someone about it, especially when I told her I was Adrian's friend."

"What did you ask her?"

"As they say in Hollywood, 'to take a meeting.' " Margaret sat back down and winked at her friend. "It's the best way to find out what Adrian was up to, don't you think?"

# 9

Margaret looked around the busy coffee shop and was totally lost. Lunchtime in an Upper West Side restaurant was bad enough; lunchtime in mid-town Manhattan was a nightmare. There must have been over a hundred people in the large restaurant, another dozen waiting for tables, and no fewer than five waiters scurrying around with loaded trays. She scanned the faces of all the people again, trying to pick out Barbara Fleischer, but it was no use. There were several women sitting alone, and nothing to indicate which of them was the Divinity editor. Margaret was just getting ready to go up to each one and ask when she felt a hand on her elbow and turned around. A woman, perhaps in her late fifties, was standing next to her with a pleasant smile on her face.

"Mrs. Binton?"

Margaret returned the smile and threw in a little nod for good measure.

"I'm sitting over there, just past that post. I saw you in the mirror looking a little confused. I took a chance it was you. I'm Barbara Fleischer." She motioned for Margaret to follow and led the way to the table. When they were seated, the editor leaned closer towards Margaret. "I have meetings all day for our sales conference, so this is the only time I could find to see you. It's supposed to be only a half hour break."

"Then I'd better order quickly," Margaret said as a waiter came by. She asked for a liverwurst sandwich on rye toast with lettuce, tomato, and horseradish sauce, and a glass of iced tea. Then she sat back to look at the other woman.

"You were Adrian's friend?" Barbara Fleischer said. "It's so sad what's happened, isn't it?"

"Sad is not the word," Margaret said. "Tragic. I only knew Adrian for a few months, but I liked him very much. We were in Smoke Stoppers together. He was my partner."

"I see," the other woman said, obviously not seeing at all why Adrian's Smoke Stoppers partner had been so interested in meeting with her. "And how can I be of help?" she asked, then lifted a forkful of chicken salad towards her mouth.

Margaret shifted on her seat, saw the ashtray on the table, and took out her pack of cigarettes. She carefully noted on the little scrap of paper her fifth cigarette of the day, tied everything back with the rubber band, and lit up.

"Adrian was rather secretive about his work," Margaret began. "I mean about what he was doing for you. He told me it was a book about people, but that was about all. I think . . ." Margaret hesitated, "I wonder if he was murdered because of what he was about to write." Margaret inhaled on her cigarette and looked closely at Barbara Fleischer. The other woman stopped the fork halfway to her mouth with another load of chicken salad on it.

"You are kidding," she said in amazement. "The papers had it as a random mugging."

"Don't believe everything you read," Margaret said politely.

The editor put her fork down slowly and frowned. It was

another minute before she spoke again. "But he was doing something so . . . so innocuous that you must be mistaken," she said.

"Perhaps. But then again, one never knows where a writer will go in his research." She leaned closer. "I was his friend—apparently the only one who seems to be interested in following up on this. The police are dragging their feet because they think it fits a certain profile that they are used to. I need to give them a push, something to work with."

"You?" Barbara Fleischer tried to keep the sound of skepticism out of her voice, but it leaked through, nonetheless. She continued to look at Margaret's lined face and gray hair pulled tightly into a bun.

"Call it volunteer work," Margaret said. "Some older women do bake sales; I help the police catch criminals, especially when they've done something to a friend." She sat back and allowed the waiter to place her sandwich in front of her. "So," she continued after the waiter had left, "could you tell me what he was working on for Divinity Publishing?"

"I don't believe this," Barbara Fleischer said, and looked around the coffee shop as if someone would come over and say "cut" to end the scene. But no one came, and her glance came back to rest on Margaret's face. She took a breath, shrugged, and started speaking.

"As you may or may not know, Divinity Publishing is a house devoted to publishing books on Christianity and related religious themes. Adrian had contracted to do a book on one church in the city, St. Martin's, which this year is having its centennial. His book was supposed to be a celebration of its one hundred years on the block, both a history of its successes in the community, and a study of its current ministrations to its multicultural congregation. The title of his book was *A St. Martin's Centennial,* and he was going to record everything he could about the beneficial changes in people's lives brought about by the church. I guess you could say that it was going to be a case study of how religion works right here in New York, a place many people elsewhere view as a twentieth century Sodom." She took a sip of water. "We at Divinity have been noticing a particularly discouraging trend in America, and we felt that this book would fit in nicely. Besides, Adrian convinced me it could also be a serious sociological study of our city in the early nineties with many threads interweaving throughout. He very much wanted it to be anecdotal; little stories that continued for a year, and of course, he wanted it to be somewhat representative of people in general. City people. He talked about that at length, about how important it was to find both welfare recipients and chief executive officers going there. And of course," she smiled, "St. Martin's has just that. It has reached out truly to the entire community."

"That doesn't sound so innocuous. It sounds very much like a writer could get carried away with some of the stories," Margaret said.

The other woman shook her head. "Oh no. Adrian was scrupulous about one thing. He was going to do this as a reporter, an observer, someone who in no way would be pejorative. That would have made people distrustful, he said, and he wouldn't have gotten their stories. And besides, he was only going to be writing about the successes, you know, the up from under sort of thing. We were very strong on that point."

Margaret thought about that for a moment. "What if in his study he came across a crime, or something dangerous that needed to be reported?"

Barbara Fleischer smiled thinly. "He assured me quite simply that it would not affect him. He knew what we were interested in, and of course, if something compromised the church it simply would not have been published. Not that he didn't have opportunities. Apparently there is at least one drug dealer going to St. Martin's who already spoke to him about his business. After all, Adrian was rather engaging. But Adrian also knew that the biggest part of his advance—and I might add that it was a pretty handsome one for a young

51

writer of his limited history—was dependant on submitting something we could accept.''

Margaret started on her sandwich and thought about what Barbara Fleischer had said. She knew writers were peculiar, but Adrian had locked himself into something morally suicidal. No wonder he smoked three packs a day. After a moment she looked back up. ''You were in touch with him as the project went on?''

''Only occasionally. We have a big list and I have about twenty books I'm currently shepherding through production. The publishing business has also been hit with belt-tightening. Year by year we're given more work, and it doesn't leave much time for creative development, or even hand-holding with writers with ongoing projects.'' She took a sip of water and continued. ''But Adrian would call maybe once a month just to tell me that everything was progressing. He couldn't start writing the current section until the year was over anyway, which I believe was sometime last week.''

''So he'd go out every day and look at the activity in the church and then interview people?''

Barbara Fleischer nodded. ''He did tell me he found this section more interesting. The historical part he submitted a few months ago, but it was only going to be the first chapter of the book. And I think he had his group of people he was tracking. It took him a while to narrow things down.''

Margaret took another bite of her sandwich, then put it back on her plate and pushed it away. ''Where is St. Martin's?''

''It is on Eighty-seventh Street between Columbus and Central Park West; nearby, but not on the same block where he lived. I think he wanted to separate his work from his life.''

''Well, he didn't do such a great job, did he? Someone got angry enough, or scared enough, and all his good intentions of sticking with the 'up from under,' as you put it, didn't keep him from getting stabbed.''

''You can't be sure of that,'' Barbara Fleischer said. A

slight color was rising into her face. Margaret hadn't spelled it out, but the subtext was certainly that Divinity Publishing had some responsibility here. And it looked like Barbara Fleischer, being a good editor, had picked up on it. "Adrian never hinted at any problems like that."

"When was the last time he spoke to you?"

Barbara Fleischer looked at her watch and motioned for the check. "I guess it was maybe two weeks ago. Certainly no longer than three weeks." The waiter came over and floated a green stub of paper onto the table. "He told me he was very excited about starting the writing soon, and that he had a lot of great material. Nothing at all about a personal threat. I really do feel you're being too . . . imaginative, Mrs. Binton. This was a religious book on love and spirituality, nothing more sinister than that." She laid a few bills on the table and stood up. "You'll excuse me," she said. "I have to get back to our meetings. Sorry I couldn't be of more help."

"One more thing," Margaret said quickly. "Did he give you anything other than his chapter on the history of the church? Any sample essays he'd sketched out about the people?"

"Nothing. I know he took a lot of notes, but then I think he transcribed everything onto a computer. He told me a good part of his first advance went into purchasing it when he saw the mountains of paperwork he was generating." She smiled thinly, excused herself again, and turned away, leaving Margaret alone with her half-finished sandwich. She could see other people waiting by the door for the table, but, Margaret figured, why rush things? How many power lunches did she get to go to anyway? Finally, twenty minutes later, she left.

No limousine was waiting, so she took the IRT train back uptown. There was nothing more she could do until that evening, so she decided to take a stroll down Eighty-seventh Street to see St. Martin's Church. Maybe she'd speak to the priest if he was in. God knows she'd passed that place a thousand times without its name even registering. But, of course, now she'd have a hard time forgetting it.

# 10

And so in conclusion," Professor Guyers was saying, "what does *Reisch versus Cosgrove* tell us?" He looked around the small room at the attentive students. Margaret was about to offer an opinion when the woman in the dashiki shot her hand into the air.

"Never trust a lawyer with money."

There were little chuckles from the other people, including from Guyers, a lawyer himself. "That too, perhaps," he said, "but what moral or ethical principal was explored in this case?" He pushed the small laptop computer away from the edge of the table and stood up. "We've spent the last half hour going over the two trials. . . ." he paused, looked down at the man with the yarmulke, and then continued. "And what is it that appears as a consistent strategy with the defense in both cases? You're a scholar, Mr. Jacobs, what struck you as being unethical here?"

The man with the yarmulke shrugged. "I guess if I had to point to something I'd say intimidation."

Guyers smiled. "Exactly. And what was so particular about Eleanor Cosgrove that makes this case such a bellwether in the study of legal ethics?"

"She was eighty-nine years old," Margaret said after a short pause from the other student. "And she was systematically harassed, frightened, and confused by the defense, as most old people would be under similar circumstances."

Guyers nodded. "Yes, thank you, Mrs. Binton. Unfortunately a typical strategy with witnesses who are of advanced years. In this case, it was clear that her lawyer, Erich Reisch, had stolen her one hundred and twenty-nine thousand dollars, and bought himself a Cadillac, some real estate, and CDs with the funds. And yet the defense so confused Mrs. Cosgrove, and impugned her memory that was, at eighty-nine years of age, somewhat inconsistent, that it took two juries to find in her behalf. The question here is whether the defense attorney acted ethically if he knew that she was telling the truth but also knew he could make her seem, because of her age, unbelievable in front of a jury. Don't forget, early on in the first trial, she is quoted as saying that she was, 'scared to death.' " He paused to take a breath. "And in his questioning it is apparent that Reisch's lawyer concentrated only on making Mrs. Cosgrove's testimony suspect, basically what I would call a cheap-shot defense. But is it unethical?" He looked around again at the class. "That is for you to decide. I would like each of you to work out that question and submit a written argument for me next class. No more than five pages, please." He smiled and looked at his watch. "And now, I think it's just about time to close. For any of you who might want to do more research on this case on your own, you will find it in," he looked down at his computer screen, "re Reisch, 101 A.D.2d 140, 474 N.Y.S. 2d 741." A few people copied the numbers down as Guyers folded the computer screen onto its case and turned off the switch. "Have a pleasant, ethical week," he said, and sat back down.

Margaret waited patiently as all of the other students

filed out of the room. In five minutes she was alone with Guyers, who was about to get up and put on his jacket.

"I wonder," Margaret began, "if I could ask you a huge favor." She smiled her most winning smile and took a few steps closer to him.

"Huge favors make me nervous," Guyers said. "How about just a normal size one." He leaned back in his chair. "I should be able to do that for one of my best students. What do you need, someone to look over a will or apartment lease?"

"Actually, no. It has nothing to do with law." She bent down and lifted up a well-used cloth shopping bag. "I wonder if you could show me how to use this damn thing. I think it's just like yours, or at least very similar." She removed Adrian's laptop computer and put it on the table between them. "I can't tell you how important it is to me."

Guyers looked down at it, up at Margaret's expectant face, then back down at his watch. "That's like trying to explain Constitutional law in a commercial break. I'm afraid it's going to take more time than I have. I usually don't eat dinner until after class."

"I thought that might be the case," Margaret added. "So I made you a nice brisket sandwich on fresh rye bread. I also have a thermos of hot mushroom barley soup." She fished the thermos and plastic container out of the bag. "Home-made," she added. "You won't get it better at Reuben's."

Professor Guyers looked at the offering, then back down at the two computers.

"Why is it so important?" he asked.

"I'll tell you," she said, "as the need arises." Then she began setting a little place with a napkin, soupspoon, and plastic bowl for his dinner.

# 11

It's a DOS machine, just like mine, so it shouldn't be a problem," he said twenty minutes later. The soup and sandwich were gone and Guyers had just finished giving Margaret a string of compliments on her cooking. "I don't think I should go into the theory of DOS. I'll just write down the commands you'll need. First of all, this switch turns it on."

"That's about all I know."

"Now, first we'll want to look into the directory. See if you can follow this." He pushed some buttons, leaned closer, pushed some more buttons, then turned the screen so she could see it. He scribbled some commands on a piece of paper as he said, "Here's the directory; now what are we looking for?" Margaret scrutinized the letters on the screen. Everything looked incomprehensible to her. Words like CONFIG and AUTOEXEC BAT stared back at her.

"I don't know. Notes, writing, the beginning of a book." She shook her head. "Some kind of information that would indicate why the owner of this computer was murdered."

Guyers looked at her and frowned. "Murdered?"

Margaret nodded.

"Okay," the law professor said and leaned back. "I too like puzzles," he added. "But I always like to start with the full instructions. Whose computer was this and how was he murdered?"

Margaret found her pack of cigarettes, slowly lifted them out of her handbag, hesitated for a few moments, then put them back.

"His name was Adrian Lavin. We were in Smoke Stoppers together. You sure you got an extra ten minutes to hear this?"

He nodded. "I have been called a casuist by my colleagues more times than I care to think about. Real life, I find, can be quite refreshing."

So she filled up the time with a complete story of why she was sitting in his classroom twenty minutes after everyone had left, trying to find a clue to Adrian's murder. When she was finished, she inspected his face to see how he was taking it.

"Makes perfect sense to me," he said at the end of her explanation. "I've been around courtrooms long enough to recognize a frightened witness when I see one. So," he shrugged, "let's see what we can find." He started pushing more buttons now, quickly glancing up at the screen, then shifting his attention back down to the keyboard. "I'm not really what the kids call a 'hacker,' but I think I can find my way around. First thing we should look at is his writing program, which I think is this one. . . ." He tapped two more buttons. . . . "WordStar. Yes, here it is. Now let's take a look at some of his files." More buttons were pushed and the screen changed through a succession of words and headings. After a moment Guyers paused and wrote down the instructions for Margaret so she could go back and forth from one file to another on her own.

"He seems to have a lot of things there," she said.

Guyers spent ten minutes calling all the small files up.

When he was finished he rubbed the back of his head and sat back.

"Mostly trash," he said. "Letters he wrote to friends, other proposals, this one here . . ." he called up one file, "is a travel article for *Travel and Leisure*. There seems to be only one large file left, almost 300 K of data. This might be it." He called up a final file Adrian had marked CRCHNOTE and together they read through the first page.

"Little anecdotes," Margaret said.

"Yes, under coded subheadings. I think this is what you're looking for. Dates, personal stories, and impressions, but it won't help you unless you find out just who these names and codes refer to. Who is lamppost, widescreen, zucchini, or firefly?"

Margaret read the last entry on the screen. "May eighteenth. Firefly told me he just sold his 1978 Skylark for eight-hundred dollars. With the money he plans a trip to Atlantic City to bankroll the car he really wants, his cousin's '85 Camaro. He needs three-thousand dollars. I asked if he ever won that much and he laughed. I also asked him how he plans to get to work without a car and he said for three or four days he'd just take the bus."

Guyers interrupted her reading. "These buttons scroll down and up the file, sort of like turning pages. You think you understand?"

Margaret nodded.

"Looks like you got a lot of material to wade through, about a hundred and eighty pages of single-spaced notes. Unfortunately, there's nothing in here I've seen so far that tells us who the code names are for." He leaned back. "Maybe you can get a clue without knowing the names. Trace things from internal information."

"With almost two hundred pages of notes?"

"I mean, after you close in on something."

"God, I'd need an army of interviewers."

"Or a lot of luck." Guyers stood up. "I wrote all the instructions down so you should be able to turn the machine off and get back into that file when you need to. That's the least I could do for that wonderful meal." He collected his papers and his own little computer and looked down at her. "I can tell, Mrs. Binton, that you are anxious to follow this up, and given that this is a class in ethics, I should encourage you. But do me a favor, don't forget the homework for next week. *Reisch versus Cosgrove.*"

"I wouldn't dream of it," Margaret assured him with a smile. "I want my A."

# 12

By the time Margaret got to the end of Adrian's notes two days later, she was exhausted and mesmerized by the wealth of detail that he had recorded. The references, cross-references, dead ends and ongoing sagas wove through Margaret's brain like a series of interrelated, three-dimensional, crossword puzzles. A picture of the St. Martin's congregation emerged, a picture very different than what Barbara Fleischer expected. It was a rendering full of petty jealousies, prejudices, vanities, and intrigues as well as loves and loyalties, interspersed amongst lives so banal as to be almost invisible. The last three pages were as typical of the entire file as any in the beginning or the middle. Margaret tackled them after her 10:00 P.M. cup of tea.

May 5th: Fanciful couldn't keep it in. She just got word that she was picked to be round-card girl for a June ring date. A friend who works with her at the beauty parlor's boyfriend is with PR at the Garden.

Big fight, maybe national TV, Manley vs. Escobel. She told me this is her big break. She figures someone's bound to see her and offer her a modeling contract with one of the agencies. She was like an eight year old with a first bike.

Picasso again. No matter how he tries, his friends suck him in. Last night they played a game of punchout on the IRT platform at 96th. (See Jan. 5th) Picasso won the pool by decking some middle-aged guy, but he thinks the guy got a good look at him. He told me he was worried since it was the first time he had played the game. On the other hand he told me it was a terrific right hand and he was glad he had won all the money. . . . $125.

Checkmate's daughter's getting married, this from his housekeeper. The boy is definitely not up to speed as per papa and he is trying to defuse the issue. Unbeknownst to him, the couple is taking off for Colorado where his uncle works right after graduation. The two of them plan to get jobs as lift operators with one of the mountains this winter and live in a camper. So much for a Princeton education. Housekeeper also reports Checkmate's liquor supply continues to dwindle as though there were holes in all the bottles. (See October 11th for Checkmate's divorce.)

Butterfly just got a promotion at work. After putting up with four years' worth of friendly pats, squeezes, and unsolicited advice from her boss she finally made asst. VP. She told me her secret. It was either sleeping with him, the way he wanted, and then getting fired, or threatening to call the guy's wife with some compromising story. The choice was clear. The guy caved in the minute she mentioned his home phone number. She and her boyfriend (see December 23rd Church Caroling) went out last night to celebrate over a bottle of champagne. He's working on a similar plan of his own with his boss who unfortunately has never stayed past 5:00 in the office.

Halo tells me things are slowing down. People are still coming into the pharmacy, still picking his brain, but sales are down. Not the Medicaid stuff—the outright purchases, impulse items like sunglasses and aftershave lotion. This keeps up he's going to have to lay off the early-shift cashier and cover it himself. Early shift is a drag, he says. That's where all the nighttime ills come home to roost. Lots of Alka-Seltzer, aspirin, antiseptic cream (cuts), Band-Aids, and gauze. The late shift is more fun. Lots of happy faces buying condoms, talcums, body oils, and mouthwash. The man certainly has a peculiar insider's view of the community.

Stroller just found out about *One Stop,* the service agency for the elderly. She's a changed woman. At eighty-six, she shouldn't have to shuttle downtown four times to get her rent increase rescinded or her homecare plan instituted. She told me they do it all for her including providing an escort service with the kids in the neighborhood. But Stroller says she's not up to being ferried around yet. Not while she's still got two good legs. She tells me her big problem is finding an extra sixteen dollars from her entitlements this month to pay for another shopping cart since the last one was stolen. Right now she's borrowing one from her neighbor (Stardust) but sometimes she's out with it all day and Stroller has to postpone her shopping. She asked me for the money but I repeated what I have said so often to all of them: I'm just a fly on the wall. Flies don't have sixteen dollars. It works both ways. Maybe they'll find her an old shopping cart at One Stop.

Ketchup was down to his last ten dollars when he finally found something. His kids were already on a diet of rice and beans (breakfast too??) when he found this job putting leaflets on the windshields of parked cars. Two cents a flier as long as he wants to stay out on the streets. Some days he comes home with fifty dollars but that's a lot of wipers to lift. His fingers are all cut from the paper and the metal but he tells me it's better than doing the can deposits for five cents each. Cleaner, not sticky, and less degrading. Only thing he tells me is they have checkers to make sure he's putting the papers on the cars and not in the garbage. He doesn't like that they don't trust him. With that and the welfare money his "wife" gets they'll just about do it. Still rice and beans, but now some chicken too.

And finally, Evergreen. She spent an hour with me this morning in the duplex after her husband left. She knows the rules but she still keeps on trying. I accepted the coffee but that's all. The doormen know what I'm doing so that's not a problem. But who knows, maybe she has a working arrangement with them. I'm sure I'm not the only one paying her morning visits. (See Evergreen, February 28th) She is not happy with the new car. The least her husband could have done, she claims, was buy the top of the line Mercedes, instead of the SX150 coupe. Looks cheesy when she drives into the club, she says, and it doesn't help her with making impressions on new people. . . . presumedly new golf pros since the report in the *Post*. Then she told me about this little Biedermeier dresser she wanted but there wasn't enough money in the account. So she went and sold the little Dufy drawing to a dealer she knows, probably got half its value, but wound up with the Biedermeier. Her husband probably won't even notice the Dufy's gone. She hung an old watercolor she took from the place in Southhampton.

Margaret took the reading glasses off her nose and wiped her eyes. Looking at this electronic print, the little flashes of light, made her eyes more tired than reading regular print. She waited a moment, then reset her glasses and scrolled the screen down. She was getting quite good at using the keyboard after two solid days of it. But there was nothing more. She had read all that Adrian had noted, this last entry day, May 19th, two days before his death. With a sigh she sat back and turned off the machine.

Next to her hand on the table was a large pile of index cards with memoranda to herself about the entries. Now she picked up her pencil and added the following questions: Call Madison Square Garden, who is ring-card girl for the Manley vs. Escobel fight (Fanciful)? Who just got divorced and had a daughter graduate from Princeton this year (Checkmate)? Which woman was just promoted to vice president at her company (Butterfly)? Is there a nearby pharmacy at the end of the block (Halo)? Who's poor, married with children, and putting flyers on cars for two cents a piece (Ketchup)? Who just got a new Mercedes SX 150 coupe (Evergreen)? Who hangs out with a particularly rough bunch of kids that plays a game called "punch-out" (Picasso)?

When she was finished she put the pencil down and looked over her index cards. They were arranged alphabetically, so it didn't take her long to insert the new ones in with the old. She already had four references to Checkmate, a half-dozen on Butterfly, one on Ketchup, and close to a dozen on Evergreen. Each collection of index cards was held together by a paper clip. In total she had eighty paper clips holding the cards together. Eighty names of people Adrian was tracking. Too much for one person, she reasoned. But then again, she had more than one person, she had all her friends from the Broadway benches to call upon. A resource waiting to be tapped if ever there was one.

# 13

ollecting all her friends together at one time was not always easy. Durso, the ex-English teacher and resident Broadway Communist was the only one Margaret could count on being present on the benches all morning. Rose, on the other hand, could be working any number of side streets, especially around the large apartment buildings near the park that always had the best trash. She'd long ago given up on the city wire-trash receptacles, since they were always picked clean by the armies of soda can retrievers. The big black bags from the apartment buildings, however, were a treasure trove of used clothing, books, utensils, and whatnots that Rose liberated for her own use. But there was no telling where she might be at ten in the morning.

And Roosa was also a problem. He might have gotten himself a bottle and not bothered to venture out at all. It all depended on the kindness of old friends in his tenement building, and on what little he could panhandle on the subways. That old devil, gin, had him in his grips, more as a willing dance partner than as a wrestling opponent.

But as Margaret approached her favorite bench at the Eighty-second and Broadway traffic island, she was happy to see he was there, grimy old peaked Midas-muffler cap in place, sunning himself and doing his best to ignore his nemesis, Berdie. While the other resident bench sitters tolerated Berdie's birds, Roosa positively hated them, hated the little noises they made that reminded him of children with popcorn stuck in their throats, hated their aggressiveness, their dirtiness, and especially hated their uniformly depressing colors. As far as he was concerned, pigeons were merely a larger, airborne version of cockroaches and he never failed to mention his feelings to Berdie. Fortunately today she was sitting on the bench across the way as Roosa's bench was full. The other people enjoying the sun with Roosa were Sid, deep into his *Daily News* racing pages, Durso, and Rena Bernstein, who was in another world listening to her Walkman.

Rena had been a saleslady at Altman's before they closed the store down, (fifteen years women's hosiery, ten years men's accessories, ten years linens, and five gift wrapping) and had spent a good forty years of her life listening to other people's needs. The first thing she did after she was pensioned off was buy herself a decent radio with earphones and zoned herself out from the rest of the daily world. She told people it was the only way she could get the memory of the constant Altman's bell paging system out of her ears. Her friends accepted her as a presence amongst them, but any conversation with Rena had to blast through her music shield on whatever radio station she was listening to. She was content to sit, sun herself, and hum a lot. One thing you could say about Rena, though, she dressed well. Forty years of Altman's employee discounts did not go to waste, and although what she wore was sometimes decades old, it was all of good quality.

Not so Pancher Reese's wardrobe. He wore the same thing each day, a white T-shirt and a baggy pair of trousers held up by the same pair of suspenders. On his head rested the same battered fedora Margaret had met him wearing years earlier. For a thin man, this outfit made him look something like an aging Norton in "The Honeymooners." Especially with the hat. Today he was sitting next to Berdie, politely holding her bag of bread crumbs. Berdie and Pancher had that special relationship that exists between two shy people who had made peace with their inhibitions and felt comfortable with each other. The fact that he still spoke with a Polish accent (née Resowski, and changed when he came to America thirty-five years earlier), and was the janitor of two of the smaller brownstones on West Eighty-first meant little to Berdie. She just liked the fact that as long as everything was running smoothly with his buildings and his sidewalk was swept clean, he usually spent an hour a day on the benches. Berdie liked talking with him, especially when Roosa was around and making nasty remarks about her birds. Pancher was so . . . polite. Just what you wanted in a friend.

Margaret found a spot next to Berdie and sat down. Just about everyone was here, everyone except Rose, but she would come to eat her lunch on the benches and Margaret would fill her in then. She put her handbag down on the bench with a dull thud and leaned closer to Berdie.

"Think you could get everybody together, you and Pancher?" Margaret said.

Berdie raised her eyebrows, or what she had penciled in as replicas. "It's about Adrian?"

Margaret nodded.

Berdie stood up and motioned across the street. "Let's go, Pancher. You'll have to help me convince Roosa. He only moves when there's a beer within reach." They crossed the street, and Margaret watched as they talked to the four others. In a few minutes the whole bunch was squeezed together on the bench, seven people who had collectively over half a millennium of life experiences, enough, one would think mistakenly, to keep them civil to each other.

"What's this craziness all about, Margaret?" Sid said. He looked at his watch. "Right in the middle of my handicapping time."

"Why don't you just give all your money to charity instead of to the bookies?" Durso asked. "Might do someone some good."

"All you pinkos ever think about is giving away other people's money," Sid growled. "Marx had it all figured out, except for one thing—he forgot that people like to have fun."

Durso turned red and was about to answer when Margaret threw out her hands. "Hold it," she said raising her voice. "You want to bicker like little school children, do it on your own time. I need help from adults." She looked around. "A lot of help. Now, shall we continue, or should I go to the center and ask there? How about you, Rena?"

Ms. Bernstein kept looking placidly across the avenue at a point three stories up on one of the buildings. The earphones were still solidly in place.

"Rena!" Margaret shouted.

"Yes," the other woman said, somewhat startled. She brought her gaze back down to earth.

"Can you help me?"

"Help you with what?" Rena asked, taking the earphones off her head. Her lined face looked concerned as if the fact of her turning off her music wasn't enough of a clue. "You need some money?"

Margaret shook her head. "Your time. I need you to go out and do some canvassing." She looked around at the other faces. "All of you," she added. "You think you could do that, ask questions of a lot of strangers?"

"Depends," Durso said, and reached into his pocket for his old cherry pipe. "On what the questions are."

"And on what kind of strangers we're asking," Roosa piped up.

The four others nodded in agreement. "And why," Pancher added. "I'd want to know that before I went around asking a lot of questions."

"Of course," Margaret said. "And so you shall. It all has to do with a boy called Adrian, a friend of mine, and about his murder."

Around them swirled noises of grinding motors and blaring horns and tires on pavement, but there was only silence from the little traffic island. Finally Rena said rather breathlessly, "Murder?"

"Yes, and we're going to find out who did it. All of us."

"Surely you're kidding," Durso said. "Another one of your classic overstatements."

"Mr. Durso," Margaret said, sitting up as straight as she could. "I am not one given to overstatement and hyperbole, unlike some of the friends in your retired teachers' association to whom you have introduced us all. You'll find what I say is accurate. Someone was murdered, the police are dragging their feet, and I think I know how to speed things up. But I need help."

"Jesus Christ," Roosa said sarcastically. "We really have time for this?"

"Yes, I'd say we do," chimed in Berdie. "Especially you, Roosa. What else do you do all day except shine the seat of your trousers on that bench or the sleeve of your jacket on a bar?" She looked around at the others for support. "Of course we have time for Margaret. In fact, time is about all this group has."

"Berdie's right," Rena said. "And just asking questions, well, that's not very hard." She folded the earphones and put them in her handbag. "Isn't that right, Sidney?"

Sid raised his eyes up to the heavens and slapped his paper open. "Good lord," is all he said.

Margaret brought her handbag closer to her and removed the stack of index cards. "Adrian was doing a study of some of the people who went to one of the churches on the Upper West Side. The first thing we have to do is figure out who those people are. I've isolated eighty of them. There's no order to them—I mean where they live—but presumedly they all are somewhere nearby. Probably many of them live on the same block the church is on. I thought I'd divide the stack up, give each of us ten of them, and have you find out who they are. Everything's in code. For example," she lifted out one group. "This one is for Circuit Breaker. Circuit Breaker turns out to have a wife and one child, plays softball Thursday nights in a Central Park league, and works as a salesman for some store downtown called Silicon City. He also plays around when his wife's not looking, is a member of a health club on East Eighty-sixth Street, and likes to eat at a restaurant called Gravelli's." She looked at her friends. "Now this person shouldn't be too hard to find. Someone has to go down to Silicon City and ask questions, or maybe go to the health club. They're not many on East Eighty-sixth. Well, there are seventy-nine more people like this, and one of them, I think, is the murderer."

"Which church was it?" Durso asked.

"St. Martin's," Margaret answered.

"That's my church," Pancher interrupted. "I mean I go there couple of times a month. Not as much as some of the regulars, but I know Father Gilmartin."

"Ah yes, sainted Father Gilmartin," Margaret said and leaned back. "I had a meeting with him already. I'm sure he's a good priest." She shook her head. "He cares so much for his parishioners that he wouldn't consider talking about any one of them. 'Confidential,' he kept saying. And the mere mention that his church might be somehow involved in what happened to Adrian made him apoplectic." Margaret looked steadily at the thin janitor with the tired-looking face. "Now maybe, Pancher, if you could figure a way to get some names, it would certainly save time finding out who everyone is. This is a little piece of luck I hadn't counted on."

Pancher thought for a moment. "Well, there's always the annual spring book fair and flea market!" Pancher said. "The first week in June they fill the parish hall with books and whatnot, and a few weeks before they hold it, they send out notices asking for things and letting people know when it's going to be held."

71

"So?" Berdie asked.

"So," Pancher said slowly, "Someone has to stuff the envelopes." He winked. "And someone has to address them."

Margaret clapped her hands. "Wonderful. And do you suppose you might be inclined to volunteer. . . . ?"

"You bet. Maybe even this week they're doing it. And I believe it's right near an office with a Xerox machine."

"Now we're getting somewhere." She looked up and smiled. "Oh good, here comes Rose."

Six other pair of eyes turned and watched as the final member of their informal bench sitting group made her way across Broadway. She was lugging at least eight shopping bags with her, strung around her like some inflated white plastic tutu. Except Rose had the legs of a billiard table. She came across cursing out the driver that had almost clipped a broom handle sticking out of her most rearward bag.

"Goddamn crazy driver!" she shouted at the long-departed taxicab, then sat down at the end of the bench. She laid the bags down neatly, wiped her forehead with a hand-kerchief, and turned to her friends. " 'Lo everybody. Whatcha' doing over here?"

"We're over here," Sid said, looking back down at his paper, "because we're all about to become junior Sam Spades. Can you believe . . ."

"Spades?" Rose repeated. "You want a deck of cards? I think I got one in here." She rummaged in one of the bags at her feet.

"Forget it," Sid added. His finger traced down the paper over the list of horses running at Aqueduct that afternoon.

"What's he talking about Margaret? What'd I say?"

Margaret explained quickly what she had taken a longer time to tell the others. At the end of it, Rose leaned back on the bench. A cautious look came over her face, and a hand went involuntarily to brush down her gray, wispy hair.

"Oh, I don't know, Margaret. I'd be too nervous to talk to a lot of people. I don't think I'd be much good at it."

"What do you mean?" Berdie piped up. "You have no problem talking to us."

"That's different, I already know you. Besides, who'd want to talk to me?"

"Rose, you have more friends than anyone," Rena said. "I think you'd be a natural."

Rose smiled thinly. "You think so?"

Rena nodded. "I do."

"So do I," Margaret said. "Maybe put a few of your 'newer' clothes on. Besides, we need you. There are too many names here to tackle without everyone's help. Even if Pancher is lucky enough to get a list of people." She looked around. "Now I can't bully you all into agreeing to do this, but if anyone is not interested, I think now is the time to tell the rest of us. And then," she hesitated, "since you wouldn't be involved, there really wouldn't be a need to stay here with us while I divided the cards." Margaret motioned idly with her hand to the other benches where some of her friends had been. She waited for a moment, but no one moved. "Well," she took a deep breath. "That settles that. Now, here's what I've done. We all can't just run around like chickens with our heads cut off, so I've already assigned everyone a bunch of coded names." She smiled. "I had a suspicion you all wanted to help me with this. We'll meet each evening at my apartment and go over what we've found. Say at six o'clock. Maybe someone with one set of names has a lead for someone with another. Cross-referencing is important. The more talking we do with each other the better. Hopefully, we can find out who all of these people are, and then give the names to the police for them to check. That would get them to stop dragging their feet on this thing." She hesitated for a moment. "Now, how does that sound to everyone?"

"It sounds like a reasonable plan," Roosa said. "But then, reasonable things give me a headache."

"Go ahead," Rena said. "Pass the cards out. We can start right away."

"Good idea," Margaret said.

"Well, aren't you the excited one?" Durso interrupted with an edge to his voice. "There's one major problem," he added, turning towards Margaret. "What about the expense of all that checking? Phone calls and all, maybe we'd even have to coax a few names out with some well-directed grease." He rubbed his two fingers together. "This could cost each of us ten or twenty dollars. That's extra money that none of us has."

"I thought about that," Margaret said. "As far as handing money out to get information, I don't really think that's necessary. People are usually nice about that. But you're right about the calls. All the phones at the Florence Bliss Center are monitored, so that's no good." She turned to Sid. "So, I thought of a solution. I thought maybe we'd give Mr. Rossman here a chance to show us how good a handicapper he is. I propose we all chip in four dollars each—surely we can all find four dollars to part with—and let him run the thirty-two dollars into something we can use for a telephone and slush fund. . . . I guess a hundred should cover it. In the meantime we could use my phone. . . . Berdie, you have a phone too, and get reimbursed from the fund later." She leaned forward and tapped Sid on the knee. "What do you say, Sid, think you're up to it?"

Sid turned slightly pink, the color of poached salmon. After all the years of his bragging how good he did at the races, his bluff was finally being called. And Sid knew that Margaret was being very casual about the money. Four dollars was not a lot, but it was still a sacrifice to Rose, Roosa, and a few of the others.

"No problem," Sid said after a moment. "I'll run it up into something respectable."

"You're gonna trust him with all that money?" Pancher said in disbelief. "What if he loses it all?"

"A chance we have to take. Now," Margaret started handing out the index cards, "Rena, you have the first group. Berdie, this next one. . . ." As she handed out the assignments, her friends looked at the cards they had been given.

74

"Here's one," Pancher said, "whose daughter is getting oboe lessons over at Brandeis High School. I think I could follow that up."

"Exactly," Margaret said. "Some of them will be easy, but others will take more effort. I think we should set tomorrow as the deadline for all the money. That'll give Mr. Rossman enough time to figure out a plan for his day at the races. . . ."

"OTB," Sid corrected.

"OTB," Margaret repeated. "Remember, let's all meet tonight at my apartment at six. Those of you that need to use a phone, you can come with me now." She stood up. "Any questions?"

"Lunch? What about lunch?" Rose said. "I've got this bagel I just bought. . . ."

"Bring it with you," Margaret said. "Tempus fugit."

# 14

That evening at 6:00, the eight bench sitters dragged themselves to Margaret's. The small one-bedroom apartment had been hers since 1949, the year she married Oscar Binton. The furniture in the living room was the same furniture the newlyweds had purchased over forty years earlier, but the rug was new. After Oscar died eight years earlier, Margaret had looked around for something to change to make the apartment less gloomy, less haunting in its memories. Nothing wholesale, just one thing different, one thing her own. She had chosen to replace the rug, which was, amongst all the furnishings, showing its age the most; and so now the old mahogany sideboards and heavily carved walnut armchairs and chintz couch sat upon a sprightly art deco Chinese rug she had purchased from Macy's at their annual rug clearance sale. It had been a big expense for her, but at the time it had clearly cheered her up and made the whole apartment brighter. But today its ebullience was wasted on her seven friends. Each looked more exhausted than the ones before as they flopped into the couch and chairs assembled in a circle around the coffee table. A pitcher of cold water and eight glasses were in the center of the table.

"So, any luck?" Margaret asked. She looked around hopefully.

"Out of my ten, I got two," Sid said. He read off their names. "One was a superintendent of a building and the other one he knew about. Eight to go."

"I drew a blank," Durso said.

"Me too." This from Rena.

"Four." Rose smiled. "Four of my people I figured out. I decided to follow your advice, that many of the people who go to that church probably live on the same block. So I found a young man sitting on one of the stoops fixing a bicycle; turned out he knew a few of them."

"Terrific," Margaret said.

"Didn't I tell you you'd be good?" Rena said with a smile.

"Better than me," Pancher said. "I only got two. The guy who works at Silicon City was easy. I'm still trying to track down the father of the young oboe player. The other one I got from Roosa. We had a chat in the middle of the afternoon and he remembered something someone had said which fit right in. But then Roosa did good also. What'd you get, three, four?"

"Four," Roosa said. "It's amazing what you can accomplish when you're sober." He smiled at the others.

"And I got three," Berdie said. "I used my phone all afternoon. Hey, we're moving right along."

"Well, with my two," Margaret said, "that totals seventeen. And we didn't even have a full day's work. Tomorrow will be even better."

Roosa groaned. "Don't remind me. Another day of being sober."

"And another day of unexamined trash," Rose said with remorse. "You know, just last week I found a perfectly good curling iron in one of the bags."

"Something you use every day," Sid said, looking at her unkempt hair.

"Well, the plug was a little shorted out, but that's easy to fix."

"I suppose," Margaret interrupted, "we should enter all these names into the computer. It would also be a good idea, the further along we get, to brief each other on our progress, who we are looking for, what new information we have. Things that might help us help each other. Hold on." She got up and went into the bedroom. When she came back she was carrying Adrian's computer. "Sid, give me the names of the people you got. . . ." and as he did she bent down and typed them in. Then she added the names of the other ones. When she was finished, she turned the machine off and sat back.

"Anything more to add?" she asked. The room fell quiet. "All right then, don't forget your four dollars tomorrow. It's a cheap price to pay to catch a murderer."

"Ever the optimist," Durso said, and stood up stiffly. "Tomorrow then."

# 15

I s that so, Mrs. Edelston?" Rena said, and wiped her mouth with the little tea napkin that had been resting on her lap. "You have subscription tickets to the opera?"

"City Opera," the other woman added. "Tuesday nights, second balcony, row F, seat one-oh-four. Had the same seat for twenty years. Heard them all, every single one they produced. Even heard Pavarotti once, but that was when he was slumming up in Central Park." She took a sip of tea and gently put the cup back down. "It's Earl Gray. I drink that and Darjeeling and that's all. The domestic stuff is downright awful, don't you think?" She smiled and a pair of large brown eyes inspected Rena. "Yes, quite bitter. Now, just what was it you wanted to ask me? I've forgotten while I was making us the tea. Oh yes, the church. Silly of me, really, but we've had such a nice chat."

Rena took a look around the pleasantly decorated room and then brought her gaze back down to her host. "I wanted to ask you about Mr. Lavin and the church, Mrs. Edelston. I suppose you've been there a long time?''

"Not so long, maybe ten years. After my husband died my daughter convinced me it was a good church to join. Meet other people my age, do some volunteer work. Besides, she was active and the children were in the Sunday school there. Now I get to see them at least once a week.''

"I wish I had grandchildren,'' Rena said wistfully. "You're very lucky.''

The other woman nodded knowingly and took another sip. There was a period of silence for a moment, and then she said, "What about the church?''

"It's really more about Adrian Lavin. He was doing a study of some of the people there. I believe you met him?''

Mrs. Edelston fidgeted for a moment. "Well, he came to see me a few times. It was nothing special, and I gathered I wasn't the only one in this building who he was talking to. We chatted about the church, and some of the people there.''

"Would you happen to know,'' Rena asked, unfolding her notes, "if any of these sound familiar?'' She proceeded to read off the characteristics of her list of ten unknown people. Midway through, the other woman stopped her.

"That last one sounds like Helga downstairs. I mean about the cats. I've never met anyone so devoted to animals in my life. Imagine, ten cats and not a whiff of odor coming from her apartment. She is scrupulous about the litter thing.'' Mrs. Edelston sniffed, then lifted her cup again and finished what was still inside. "Besides, we walk home from church sometimes so I know it's her. Go on,'' she directed, "read me some of the others.''

Rena read two more and again she was stopped.

"Oh yes, definitely that bad actor up on five. The only one around here I don't like. What's his name again . . . Sherill, that's it. Peter Sherill. Plays loud music and dresses like some Italian gigolo. The man's got to be over forty-five if he's a day but that doesn't mean he's got the same sex appeal as Gregory Peck.'' Mrs. Edelston colored briefly. "My favorite actor. Anyway, you know how it is with some of these men. Desperately fighting against time. Middle-aged bodies with adolescent ideas." She paused for a breath. "Who else you got?"

Rena read off the last three and again got lucky. The last one in her notes was a young woman dancer.

"Dena, on the first floor," the other woman said. "Back apartment. The way she moves you can tell she's a dancer, but besides, she once put flyers downstairs for one of her programs. I went, although as you know, I like the opera better. Not bad, actually; I think she was a swan. Let's see, long dark hair—that fits—always going to exercise class, that too. With her body you should see the looks she gets from Sherill when she passes him in the hall. I've even seen her talking to Mr. Lavin now and then. So, what's that, three of them?"

"And you," Rena said. "I got your name from my friend Mr. Reese, who also volunteers at the church." Rena hesitated. "You do know," she said finally, "that Mr. Lavin was killed last week outside his apartment?"

Mrs. Edelston rose slowly from her chair. "Yes. I read about it." She took a few steps towards her door, still looking closely at Rena. "I do suppose that's why you are asking about him now, to find out and notify all of his friends."

"Yes," Rena smiled. "All his friends."

"Well, do stop in again if you're in the neighborhood. Maybe you'd like to join me one night at the opera. There are always a bunch of tickets for sale out front. Won't be as good as mine, of course, but it's such a wonderful hall it won't matter. And this year they're doing a lot of Donizetti."

"I'd like that," Rena said sincerely. "Very much. And thank you for your time." Rena closed the front door slowly behind her a minute later. Well, now she was getting somewhere, and it was only 1:30. There was plenty of time to finish up in the building. No telling what else she might find out.

* * *

81

Pancher walked slowly down the dark staircase. One would think that in such a decent neighborhood there'd be at least two bulbs per floor, but apparently the landlord was on a tight budget. The building reflected that too. The hallways looked like they had last been painted before the invention of the roller. Little blooms of graffiti sprouted on the walls like mold in a mushroom cave, and the floor had enough loose boards to make even Vincent Price comfortable. Amazing, Pancher thought, and this not fifty yards off Central Park West. If this had been the building he was taking care of he'd have been fired long ago. It was obvious that this building was being inventoried for some grander purpose, certainly not to provide pleasant residences. Of the twenty apartments, ten were empty or had people living in them of such a transient nature Pancher wondered if they'd be there the following week. Two of the people he spoke to were actually moving out that day, having found a larger place for their family. Three others had not been there longer than two weeks. But for all its seediness, some of the people he spoke to told him the building was in fact safe. Perhaps that was because it was directly opposite St. Martin's Church. Pancher had spoken to all of the tenants who opened their doors, and of them, only one seemed to fit his descriptions. The piano teacher on the top floor admitted that he went to St. Martin's and had been interviewed several times by "that writer, Mr. Adrian." The only lead from him was that the man living in the basement had also been known to frequent the church on occasion.

"But he's a crazy artist," Gideon Stokes, the piano teacher had said, "who makes strange noises in the night. You wouldn't want to see him."

But Pancher did, and was a little nervous now as he stepped down into the dimly lit basement hallway.

The first thing he heard were the strange loud noises, almost as though someone was beating against a radiator. Except it was tinnier, the sound of sheet metal. At first Pancher rapped on the door tentatively, but when he realized he hadn't been heard he banged with the side of his hand.

The noises from within stopped, and a moment later the door opened. Standing in front of Pancher was a man of medium build in a T-shirt that looked like it had been through electroshock therapy. The edges were frayed, the neck was charred, and tiny burn holes permeated the fabric everywhere. The man's blue jeans were a good match to the shirt and even his shoes showed tiny scars. Pancher looked into his eyes, or looked into where his eyes should have been, but saw only welding goggles. The other man inspected him through the goggles for a moment, then gave him the courtesy of removing them. An oval of lighter color, unsmudged skin surrounded the dark eyes and made him look like a human badger.

"Yeah?" he asked curtly. Obviously Pancher, in his suspenders and T-shirt and hat did not look official.

Pancher took a quick glance over the other man's shoulder into a room that looked more like a garage than an apartment. Steel racks held lengths of steel pipe and angle iron, shelves held thicknesses of sheet metal, and one wall was covered with bins of odd metal shapes and parts. The linoleum had been removed from the floor, which now held thin metal plates, the kind Pancher had seen on loading docks around town. The acrid smell of burning oil and solvents wafted out and surrounded him on the small basement landing.

"You live here?" Pancher blurted out before he had a chance to stop himself.

"Yes, I live here, in the back. Who are you?"

"My name's Reese, Pancher Reese," the older man recovered. "I'm not an inspector if that's what you're thinking. But I have a couple questions I'd like to ask you?"

"What about?"

"Adrian Lavin and his church project. You're Lorenzo Tyler, right? A man upstairs gave me your name."

The other man remained silent for a moment, nodded, then stood aside. As Pancher passed by him, he took off his goggles and welding gloves, and lit a cigarette.

83

"Unlucky bastard," Tyler said.

"I don't think luck had anything to do with it," Pancher said, and looked around for someplace to sit. He found a stool, brushed off the top, and hiked himself up. He found himself facing a wall of garish, bizarre steel masks, each one looking like the head of some alien insect, all different; antennae and mandibles and maxillae reaching out at crazy angles. They were unpainted, showing off the rough steel in all its hammered and welded roughness. Primitive, but impressive as a body of work, expressing a vision that was unique and peculiarly fitting. A gallery of enlarged urban roaches was what Pancher thought. He studied them for a moment, then asked the young artist if he knew Lavin well.

"Well enough," the artist said. "I spoke to him maybe once a week. I knew he was doing some kind of research thing, with the people in the church, but he also liked to come and see the new work."

"Did he talk much about the other people he was writing about?"

Tyler shook his head. "He was very closed about that." The young man took a last drag on the cigarette, then dropped it on the floor where it remained glowing. A dozen other cigarettes lay surrounding it; some of them looked to be burned-down joints. "But then I didn't care," the young man continued. "It gets pretty empty down here sometimes during the day. I kind of like talking to people now and then. And besides, Adrian was a good interviewer."

"Meaning?"

The artist hesitated. "Meaning that he had a knack for finding out things."

"Maybe that's what got him in trouble," Pancher said lightly.

"Not with me. We had a good relationship. That's one of the things he found out. I'm easy to deal with."

Pancher looked him full in the face and took a long shot. "What were you dealing?"

The artist's face broke into a smile. "Look around you,

pop. How do you suppose I support this noble artistic career? Steel cost a lot these days. I'll give you a hint; it wasn't insurance.''

"Something else Mr. Lavin found out?"

The artist looked surprised. "Hell no, I told him. Like I just told you. I'm not bashful." He winked. "Just careful. I pick my spots. Looking at you I'd say there was little chance you were working for the local drug enforcement task force. Who knows, you might even want to try some yourself."

Pancher shook his head. "No thanks, but what about Adrian? Did he buy stuff from you?"

The artist shook his head. "His drug of choice was nicotine. We left it at that."

Pancher leaned back on the stool and nodded. After a moment of thought he continued. "You have any idea why someone would want to kill him?" he asked.

"No, as far as I could tell he was friendly with everyone. He used to walk people home from church, go to some of their events with them."

"I see," Pancher said, and slowly reached into his pocket. "You mind telling me if anyone here sounds familiar?" He read through his list of index cards, omitting the people he'd already identified, but the other man couldn't add anything.

"Sorry," he said.

Pancher got up to go. He took a last look at the masks, then turned towards the door.

"You know, Mr. Tyler, these masks, they're real good. I used to do some welding, but I could never dream up the things you have. But, if I were your father, I'd make you move into a healthier place soon as I could." He shook his head. "And dealing, that's not smart."

The artist laughed. "Thanks, pop. I'll remember that." He opened the door and stood aside as Pancher left. Then he lowered his goggles back over his eyes and went back to his steel fantasies.

# 16

What an incredible piece of good luck, Sid thought as he walked into the polished marble lobby of 258 Central Park West. There in front of him, dressed in the uniform of a doorman, was Dominick Spina, one of his buddies from OTB. That airless, smoke-filled parlor of handicapping had spawned many a friendship, most of them extending only as far as its four walls. One of them had been between these two men. They chatted, sometimes for hours on end, not knowing any detail about the other person except his love of horseflesh, betting, and stuffy spaces. They had seen each other for years inside the OTB on Ninety-first Street, had exchanged tips, argued track conditions, debated jockeys, not once knowing where the other person lived or what they did. And now, here was Dominick walking towards him with his doorman cap and thick glasses, about to ask him for a name so he could announce him to some tenant.

"Hey, Dom, who you like in the third?" Sid asked jokingly. He shot the cuffs on his houndstooth jacket just like he did when he was making a point at OTB.

The look he got from his friend was a mixture of surprise and annoyance. Spina quickly looked around to make sure no one had overheard.

"Hey Sid, what're you doing here? Visiting someone?"

"Maybe," Sid said. "I didn't know you worked here."

"Yeah, we all got to pay the rent somehow. I hope you didn't come to talk horses because I'm kinda busy."

Sid was about to say something when a middle-aged woman walked up and broke abruptly into their conversation.

"Dominick, I'm expecting my decorator, Gabriella, around two o'clock today. You can let her upstairs. She has a key." Without waiting for a response she turned on her heel and walked out the front door. Dominick touched the brim of his cap and fired off a crisp "yes, Mrs. Dusatoy" in response.

"It's like that, is it?" Sid asked with a grin.

"Still too early for retirement," his friend said. "Another two years of this crap, then I'm on my pension." He took off his glasses and wiped them. "So what the hell you doing here, Sid?"

"I gotta find out if someone lives in this building. It's either this one or the one on the northwest corner." He gave a description of the woman "Evergreen" and of the Mercedes SX150.

"Yeah, that's Nancy Sherwin in fourteen-B. I recognized her by the car and the place in Southhampton."

Sid grinned with success. "You got time for a few more?"

"I guess so."

Sid ran through his index cards quickly and got lucky a second time.

"The one you call "Moon" is Gil Morper in three-D. Low floor, small back apartment. Young stock player with a tip a day. Works for some independant stock brokerage firm on lower Broadway. You know I sort the mail every morning,

I get to know a lot about my tenants." He grinned at his OTB buddy and continued. "So what's this all about, anyway? You doing a survey?"

Sid told him about Adrian; not everything they were doing, but enough to get a response.

"Yeah, I remember the guy. Came in here a lot. Sure, Sherwin and Morper, and occasionally one or two others he'd go to see."

"I'm surprised he didn't concentrate on interviewing you, Dominick."

"Who said he didn't?" the other man asked. "Once a week, like clockwork. He threw me a little something and I told him a lot."

"And was he interested in everyone?"

The doorman shook his head. "Un unh. He had a list of people who went to the church. Then out of those, he was only interested in the people with stories. . . ."

"Stories?"

"You know, interesting problems. The people who were just regular slugs he'd speak to maybe once, then never go back. The ones that had stories he'd latch onto."

"So Sherwin and Morper had 'stories'?"

Dominick nodded. "You bet. You want to hear what I told Lavin about Morper?" He lowered his voice.

Sid nodded.

"An illegal alien. His real name is Morpenzo. I think he's from Mexico, or maybe Guatemala. Not your usual wetback, but one just the same. I think he was a student whose visa ran out, but not before he had made a pile of money investing nickels and dimes in the biotechs a few years ago. He told me about a few companies, but hell, betting a mudder at Aqueduct in April is one thing, investing in a dinky little gene splicer in Sacramento is quite another."

"How do you know he's here illegally?" Sid asked.

"I can spot it. He's only been here for half a year, but already he's gotten lots of letters from organizations called Human Rights and Legal Assistance Fund, and South American Alliance for Immigration Reform, and a bunch of things from the Department of Immigration and Naturalization. Come on Sid, wake up and smell the Sanka. He's probably trying to find a way to stay here, some little loophole."

"And you told Lavin that?"

The other man nodded. "I figured the young kid was okay. He told me he'd keep everything confidential. Besides, Morper saw him several times so they must have hit it off."

"How'd you know his real name was Morpenzo?" Sid asked.

"Because the first week he came down and told me if I see any mail for Morpenzo to send it up. Most of the stuff that comes in under that name comes from Mexico, some from Guatemala. Personal letters. Like from family."

"So, he changed his name. Big deal." Sid shook his head. "Could be nothing." Sid thought for a moment. "And Nancy Sherwin?" He raised an eyebrow.

"That one's easy. What's a word that describes someone who gets daily visits from a lot of different, strange men?"

"You're kidding? In this building?"

"Hey, I'm sure she ain't cheap."

"But you said she's married."

Dominick laughed. "Sid, stick to handicapping horses. I think you're out of your league picking women."

Sid was silent for a few moments. "Are either of the two in now?" he finally asked.

The doorman Dominick shook his head. "She goes out for lunch, maybe returns at three. Morper gets back after five."

Sid took another tack. "Was there anyone else Lavin was interested in in the building? Someone with a 'story' but not on my cards?"

"One other. A lawyer name of Winterspoon. He'd see him also once a week."

Sid listened for a few minutes while Dominick gave details about a man from 12A.

"I think he's on Roosa's list. Maybe Checkmate."

Dominick looked askance. "What're you working for, some goddamn detective agency? You surprise me, Sid."

"So, you ever tell me you were a doorman?" Sid said sarcastically. "How do you find the time to go to OTB anyway?"

"I get out of here at three. Plenty of time for the late races. In fact, I got something good for today's seventh," he winked, "and I think I got something extra special for later in the week."

Sid smiled, warming to his favorite subject. "I'm open to suggestion," he said.

Just then Mrs. Dusatoy walked back into the building and once again came straight over to Dominick. She was holding a garment on a hanger with some plastic over it.

"Send this dry cleaning right up, Dominick," she said. "Tell my housekeeper it goes with my winter clothes. In the back hall closet." Once again she turned and left without waiting for a response. This time Dominick didn't offer one.

"The back hall closet," Sid mimicked. "God forbid it should go in the bedroom closet with the autumn wardrobe." Dominick made a face and turned to deliver the dry cleaning. Sid followed. "So, you were saying you had something special later in the week?"

"I'll see you later," the other man called over his shoulder. "You probably got too many things on your mind right now."

"Come on. Just give me the name. I'll do the checking myself."

Dominick hesitated, then nodded. "Okay then. Hairy's Pride. In the fifth on Thursday. I can't tell you, but I got it real reliable."

"Thanks," Sid said, and turned to the door. "See you later."

"Should I tell those people you're coming back?"

"No," Sid said. "Don't tell them anything."

# 17

It was such a nice evening that Margaret decided to move the meeting out of doors. The benches on Broadway were too noisy, so the whole flock of them left her apartment and walked over to Riverside Drive. It was one of those warm spring evenings welcomed by everyone, especially after a damp week. They found an empty bench, and the eight of them crowded together.

"Hot," Rose said, fanning herself with a piece of cardboard.

"Whyntcha take off one of your five layers," Roosa said. "It's nice out here without all that insulation."

Rose shook her head. She had herself pieced together just right, and removing a treasured article of clothing was more difficult for her than just waving the scrap of folded pizza box. "It's gonna get chilly tonight," she said, "and then I'll just have to search for where I put it." She fanned herself a few more strokes, then turned to Margaret with a smile. "I got all my people. Every last one." Her smile turned into a little mischievous grin and she looked back at Roosa. "How'd you do?"

"Two to go," he said, and reached for his list.

"One," Sid amended. "I think I found you Checkmate."

Pancher pulled a list out of his pocket with a flourish.

"Here, this is what I did. Better late than never. I think it's about half the names from the church's mailing list. I put in a few hours mailing envelopes this morning before tracking down some of my people."

"Wonderful." Margaret beamed. "This will help a lot. How about the rest of you?"

The others reported on their successes. When it was all tallied up it appeared they had only twelve more names to ascertain from Adrian's original eighty.

"Maybe we can finish it all tomorrow, especially with Pancher's list."

"Then what?" Berdie asked. "This has been kinda fun. I met someone today who keeps parrots in her apartment. Ten of them. The place sounded like a kindergarten class, all of them talking at once, no one listening. One sings like Vic Damone, another recites the Declaration of Independence. I can't wait to go back." The others were silent. "Well, the lady said I could, and bring anyone else I wanted." Berdie looked around at her friends, but there were no takers.

"Then we give the names to the police!" Margaret concluded. "They have ways of finding out things that we don't. Asking about where people were the night Adrian died. Applying pressure. If we tried that, they'd just laugh at us."

"Eighty's a lot of names," Sid said. "You sure they'd do it?"

"They better," Margaret said. "It's a good chance one of them is the murderer. Now," she leaned back, "a new topic. What about the money? So far Berdie and I have spent hours on our phones. It's four dollars each, remember. Sid's going to show us all how good he is."

Grudgingly all the people on the bench reached into various pockets, pouches, purses, and wallets and came up with the money. Sid wound up with thirty-two dollars in singles, each bill looking like a miniature used dish towel. He stuffed everything into his jacket pocket and looked at the others. They were looking back as if he were carrying the Message to Garcia.

"I got a hunch for the day after tomorrow, Thursday," he said. "How much you need, Margaret? A hundred?"

"That would be nice," she smiled. "Wouldn't it be, Berdie?"

The other woman nodded. "Very nice."

Margaret stood up. "As I said, with any luck we'll be finished tomorrow," she said. "I'll call Lieutenant Morley, get hold of the right people to give the information to, and we can go back to being our old selves again. Although I do admit, like Berdie, this has been diverting. It's sad that Adrian never finished the book. It would have been an interesting read."

"Indeed," Durso said. "Interesting enough to kill for."

# 18

Two days later, at precisely one-thirty in the after-noon, Margaret Binton marched into Lieutenant Morley's office with a large manila envelope under one arm, and a tightly sealed small tin box under the other. She placed both of them on top of a stack of papers on his desk and sat down in her favorite chair, the one with the wooden arms and Naugahyde back. Morley looked at her over the rim of his glasses with as patient an expression as he could muster. But then she had caught him at a good time. He had just received the new budget for the month and was surprised to see that only two patrols were being canceled. He had been prepared, with all the austerity talk, to be giving pink slips to at least a half-dozen men.

"So," he began, "let me guess. You came in on that Lavin thing. You'll be happy to hear that I called up Homicide and they put a few more people on it. Green and Edwards, I think he said their names were. To be honest, though, I've been so busy I haven't followed up or heard anything yet."

He flipped the glasses up to the top of his head. "But I bet that's why you're here."

"Yes," Margaret said. "That too. But," she leaned forward and took the tin out from under the yellow envelope, "first things first. I should have been here earlier this morning, but I was busy with these. I figured I'd soften you up first." She handed the box across the desk. Morley took it and felt its weight.

"Lemon pecan or molasses raisin?"

She shook her head. "I thought I'd try something different, something healthy. They're oat bran crunch."

Morley made a face in spite of himself.

"Go ahead and try one. They're good."

He pried the lid off and peered inside. "They look disgustingly healthy." He lifted out one of the cookies and bit into it. "Not bad, but I'd hate to think what these would taste like on a humid day." He finished the cookie and put the top back on the box. "Okay, I'm ready," he said with a grin. "You've softened me up. I'll place the call and ask where they are with it."

"Tell them I have the name of the murderer," Margaret said. "In there." She nodded in the direction of the envelope. "The problem is, along with the murderer's name, there are seventy-nine others. Your people are going to have to weed it out."

Morley leaned back in his chair. "You want to explain? I mean, maybe fill me in a little so I don't sound like such an idiot on the phone when I call Renzuli down at Homicide."

"It's just like I told you," she said. "It's got to be someone he was interviewing for his book, so after four days with eight of us working, we found out who they were. All of them, I think. The rest is up to your people." She pushed the envelope closer to Morley. "Here are the names and addresses. No charge. Just take it from here."

Morley nodded slowly. "That simple, huh?"

"Why not?"

"Well, let's see," Morley said. "Most heads of departments like Renzuli don't like being told how to do their job. Then, using civilians to do basic police legwork is the kind of thing defense attorneys love. You do anything illegal in getting these names?''

"Illegal? We all just asked people around the neighborhood. First people on the same block with the church he was researching. . . .'' She hesitated, wondering whether to tell him about the partial list Pancher had gotten. "Then others we found out about. That's all.''

Morley sighed and leaned back. "Let's hope Renzuli's open to suggestion. You understand, Margaret, this is not in my court anymore. I can just suggest . . .''

"I understand. Make the call. I'll listen in on your end.''

He took another look at the box of cookies, and lifted the receiver slowly. In a minute he was connected through to Lieutenant Renzuli.

"Tony,'' he began. "This is Morley over in the Eighty-first. I'm calling about Lavin. You have anything yet?''

Morley was usually good at controlling his expression, but something Renzuli said must have been a shocker. Margaret saw his forehead wrinkle, and then slowly Morley lifted the glasses off his head and placed them on the top of his desk.

"What?'' he said, almost in a whisper.

There was silence in Morley's office for almost a minute, and then he spoke again.

"Did he confess?''

Margaret took a deep breath and put her hands on the wooden arms of her chair. The motion was involuntary, almost as though she had been dropped from a great height and had to hold on to something firm. For the next few minutes Morley nodded and said a few "yeahs" and "uh huhs" into his phone, but mostly he listened. Margaret tried to catch his attention, but he was not looking at her; he was looking at the manila envelope in front of him.

"Are you sure?'' he asked finally, and looked at last in her direction. "Okay, thanks,'' he added. "Let me know.''

Just as slowly as he had lowered his glasses, he now lowered the phone onto its cradle.

"Well?" Margaret asked, feeling a tightening sensation in her stomach. "Don't tell me they have someone yet?"

"Signed, delivered, and almost sealed. No confession yet, but the guy's still wacked out on crack. When he comes down, Renzuli is confident he can jog his memory."

"And the story so far?" Margaret asked.

"He tried mugging some guy over on Riverside Drive who was a little faster and luckier than Adrian. Kicked the knife out of the way, then busted his nose for him. A karate expert or something. When the cops searched him they found, among other things, Adrian's wallet. No money, of course, but credit cards galore. Pretty open and shut, Renzuli thinks."

"Was it someone from the neighborhood?"

Morley shook his head. "A guy with a long record. Muggings, robberies, assaults. Couple of years here, couple of years there. A hard core with more time in the pen than out. Last known address was somewhere in Brooklyn. Name of Melendez, Hector Melendez."

Margaret released the arms of her chair and eased herself back. She turned her head slightly sideways and looked at the lieutenant out of the corner of her eyes, a trait she fell into whenever she was dealing from skepticism.

"It will not work," she said slowly. "Not with me, and it shouldn't with you either."

"Melendez fits the description given of the man running away from Lavin's building the night he was killed. Short, dark hair, little mustache, sneakers, slightly overweight."

"That's the description of half the people on the Upper West Side. Doesn't prove a thing."

"Prove? No," Morley said, "but it sets things in motion. Renzuli is going after him like a terrier, and I guarantee he won't let go until he shakes something loose. In the process, he won't be interested in much else. He's working up an expanded sheet on Melendez, getting his people to canvass

97

again with his picture, checking on the similarity of the weapons, where they were bought, etcetera and like that." Morley paused and looked again at the manila envelope. "He's not going to look at that now."

Margaret had felt it coming, but still she was angry.

"Eight people spend four days of their lives getting vital information and you won't even pass it on. Just because some two-bit grifter was unlucky enough to pick up a wallet, probably out of the garbage, and then get caught pulling a dumb mugging. That's what it was, probably. You must know that. You think the real murderer would be stupid enough to hold on to his victim's wallet? I'd laugh if it wasn't so pathetic. Mr. Melendez may be hard core, as you call it, but he's no murderer, at least not of Adrian."

"Unfortunately, that's not what Lieutenant Renzuli thinks, and Lieutenant Renzuli is in charge of Homicide," Morley said, with a little too much inflection in his voice. "Listen, Margaret, I can give him your stuff if that's what you want, but I don't want to disappoint you. I know how these things go. Renzuli's plate is more than full. He's probably got a dozen open murders he's working on, so when he gets a bona fide lead, that's what he chews on. If his lead doesn't pan out, well then, maybe, eventually, he'll get to what's in there." He nodded in the direction of the envelope on his desk. "If you still want to leave it."

Margaret didn't hesitate. She positioned her large handbag in the center of her lap, opened the clasp on its top, then leaned forward. In the time it took Morley to blink twice, the envelope was inside and the bag shut.

"I am not the kind of person who asks my friends to waste their time," she said. "We are of an age when that is a commodity in precious short supply." She stood up stiffly, and glowered down at the younger man. "Nor am I in the habit of wasting my own time doing favors for some weak-watered police officer with the brains of a shoelace." She turned on her heel and headed for Morley's door. "Do not trouble yourself further on my account," she continued. "I am quite capable of seeing myself out as well as seeing a project to its end."

"Margaret," Morley said, standing up also and now quite red in the face, "baking cookies is one thing, messing in police business is quite another. Here's one good piece of advice. Go back to your friends and leave Lavin's murder to us."

"Sure," Margaret said as she reached the door. "Along with a street map and the address of the nearest necromancer. You can tell Renzuli he's barking up the wrong tree. But I'm surprised you're down there baying with him." Margaret turned through the door and Morley watched as she walked down the corridor. Then he sat back down.

"Weak watered!" he said softly, ". . . brains of a shoe-lace . . . now what the hell was that?"

# 19

The OTB office was full of its normal clientele when Margaret entered later that afternoon. Unlike Saturday, when the parlor sopped up thousands of paychecks, it was possible to make it to one of the betting windows without getting pressed like a dried flower by the crush of sweaty bodies. Bodies sweated in the OTB even in December. They sweated out decisions, sweated out racing calls, sweated out how to tell the family the paycheck was gone, and even, on occasion, sweated out what to do with the winnings. Margaret disliked the place, its crush, its smells, its collection of pale, aimless people wasting their time when they should have been out in the sun. And she didn't understand how these mostly elderly people could spend even more time confronting yet another clerk behind a counter. That's all old people did, confronted Welfare, Social Security, Medicare, Housing Authority, or a dozen other grudging agency clerks on a daily basis to obtain benefits. Margaret felt there was something basically adversarial talking to someone behind a counter, especially one with a glass window.

She spotted Sid against one of the columns in the middle of the room looking up at one of the monitors. She had forgotten. When they weren't talking to clerks behind glass, everyone was watching a television tube at an angle that insured they'd have neck spasms the rest of the day. Watching dancing numbers, like they were three year olds watching Ernie or Bert do ballets with digits. Very educational. Margaret cut through the shoulders and smoke and tapped Sid on the arm.

"We have to talk," she said. "It's important."

"So is this. The fifth is about to go off."

Margaret looked up at the monitor. The screen was now showing a bunch of horses approaching a starting gate. "Come on Sid, it's just another race."

"Not just another race. Except for five bucks, all our money is on the sweet black nose of number three, Hairy's Pride. And guess what, he's the long shot. Thirty to one."

"You put our money on some horse no one wants?" Margaret peered at the monitor, trying to find Hairy's Pride. "Which one is he?"

Sid grinned. "The one on crutches."

"Very funny. You're supposed to know what you're doing here, Mr. Rossman. Being frivolous with other people's money does not seem very responsible."

"I didn't bet him to win, Margaret. I'm not stupid. Just to place." He looked at her and the grin evaporated. "Trust me."

"I have a choice?" she said, and looked back up to the screen. The horses were now in the gate, and the noise level in the OTB parlor noticeably lowered.

"The smart money's on number seven, Meadowshark," Sid said. "But it's got no price and I think this is a race for the track boys. If we come in you can get yourself a cellular telephone."

"I don't want a cellular telephone," Margaret said tightly, "just enough to pay me back for the phone calls I made and maybe to buy a few extra packs of cigarettes."

101

"Should've stopped long ago."

"You're telling me." The talk of cigarettes inspired her and she fumbled in her handbag for her works. She didn't even bother writing down what number cigarette it was; she lit it quickly and watched as the horses broke from the gate. For the first half of the race the pack of horses was so close that even the caller was having a hard time. Margaret squinted, but without her glasses and at such a distance, all she saw was a clot of darkish forms bobbing around in the center of the screen. Then one dark form started pulling away and the clot separated into two. A noise went up in the room and she could feel Sid grab her arm.

"Meadowshark is still back in the field," he shouted.

"So who's that?"

"Hairy's Pride!"

Margaret took a drag on her cigarette and took a step closer to the monitor. "Come on you son of a butcher, run!" she shouted. "Run!"

Now another horse pulled away, and then another, and then the three front-runners came around the final turn. The caller remained unemotional in his delivery, but the rest of the room was urging on their choices, along with Margaret. She swung her arm in cadence with the horses' gait and a little spark from her cigarette fell off and stung her hand. She brushed it off lightly and kept rooting Hairy's Pride on. The three horses were very close, with the one on the outside coming on strong, when they crossed the finish line. To Margaret it was all a blur. She wiped her forehead and turned to Sid.

"Who won?" she asked.

"Photo. We might be in there."

"I don't believe it," Margaret said, and put her hand to her heart. "That was . . . exciting." Her face was flushed.

"A lot more exciting if we win." Sid looked at her with a wry smile. " 'Run, you son of a butcher?' Where did that come from?"

102

"Must have just slipped out," Margaret said, looking guilty. "Oh my, when do we find out about the money?"

"When you hear the grumbling, that's when."

It took another three minutes for them to post the order of finish, and when they did there was a lot of grumbling and a few curses. Smart money hates losing. Meadowshark came in third, a nag called Enigma came in second, and good old Hairy's Pride first. Sid squinted at the payouts and quickly figured the take.

"Not bad, five twelve. Course, I've done better."

Margaret asked lightly, "Is that what I think it is? Five hundred and twelve dollars?"

"Every penny of it." He grinned. "And that's not including the exacta."

"The what?"

"The other five dollars. I took an exacta on our horse and Enigma, another long shot, the one that came in second. Boy, this really was one for the boys at the track. Let's see," he looked at the payout again, "a five dollar exacta comes to just over nine hundred. I guess all told, that should cover the phone calls and butts."

"And a lot more." She crushed her cigarette on the floor and looked back up at her friend. "And there will be a lot more. That's what I came to tell you."

Sid squinted at her. "How's that? I thought you were going to your friend Morley with everything."

"Yeah, well," she sighed. "Sometimes your friends let you down."

# 20

It could be worse," Margaret said. "It could be a hundred and sixty names." She looked around at the other faces on the bench with her. "Eighty's a snap. That's ten each. Just like before."

"Not quite," Durso pointed out. "Before we were only identifying them; now you're asking us to eliminate those we think are innocent. That's a bit more . . . creative, wouldn't you say?"

"Don't you like puzzles?" Berdie asked him. "You, of all people, Joe, the one always talking about the mystery of capitalism's appeal to the working man. Here's a chance for you to get down from your soapbox and into the real world."

Margaret held up her hand. "Now, now, Berdie, this is not the time for divisiveness. We have to stick together."

Berdie looked down at her pigeons but couldn't help showing a little grin. It wasn't often she got a good dig in at Durso, especially in front of so many people. What a pompous ass he was, anyway. He needed a little deflating now and then. She reached into her bag, threw out a handful of crumbs, then looked back up. "Sorry, Margaret. But go on, how are we going to do this?"

"Slowly. Person by person," her friend said. "First we exclude all those people that don't fit the description of the murderer. All women, tall men, black and Oriental men, old men, men with limps and ailments. Let's see where that leaves us. I bet the eighty gets down pretty fast. After that we can concentrate on those that might have had something sensitive they revealed to Adrian."

"How are you going to figure that out?" Roosa asked. "Most of the stuff on those index cards was pretty innocent."

Margaret took a deep breath. "Yes, I know, just what his editor, Barbara Fleischer, would have wanted. But, to be quite frank, something's been bothering me. Why, Sid, did your doorman friend, Dominick Spina, tell you that who Adrian was really interested in were the people with shady stories? Why, especially when he knew that none of it would have made it into the book he contracted for? And why did he go back several times to talk with Lorenzo Tyler, the drug-dealing artist, or for that matter, Mrs. Sherwin, the woman who was having afternoon assignations? These are not 'up from under' stories. And where are they, all the little compromising notes on these people? Roosa is right. What we have so far is too innocent. Not only did he give his people code names to protect them, maybe he also gave their stories, the juicy ones, protection by putting them in a safety box or something." She looked around again. "I'm beginning to think that maybe Adrian was a little more devious than I gave him credit for. Maybe he was doing two projects at once, one for Divinity Publishing, and one for himself. Is that crazy?"

"I don't think so," Pancher said. "After all, he was out to make money. What sells more, the *National Enquirer* or a puffed-up piece of self-promotion that would put a speed freak to sleep?"

"So maybe I have to go back to his apartment again?" Margaret said.

"You couldn't," Berdie said with an edge to her voice. "That place has got to be buzzing with cops now."

"I don't think it's in his apartment," Sid said slowly, and leaned back. "I think it's in yours."

"Mine?" Margaret said.

"Where everything else was, in the computer. I think you're right about the safety box, except it's not a box, it's a chip."

The eight friends were silent for a few moments. Finally Margaret said, "I didn't see it."

"No, you wouldn't," Durso added. "It's masked somehow. Maybe it's something with a password."

"Uh huh," Margaret said slowly. "I'll have to ask Professor Guyers again. But for now, why don't we go through and see how many we can eliminate."

"The money," Sid said softly. "You were going to tell them. . . ."

Margaret held her hand up and beamed. "Yes, of course. I almost forgot." She reached into her handbag and pulled out a large manila envelope. "Good news. Here's everyone's four dollars back . . . with interest." She handed out one hundred and eighty dollars to everyone. "Courtesy of our friend, and racing handicapper par excellence, Mr. Sid Rossman. Never again will I question his abilities. Take a bow, Mr. Rossman."

Sid grinned. "Was nothing, I assure you."

"Close to fifteen hundred dollars worth of nothing," Margaret said. "That should more than cover all our expenses. Any comments?"

"Just one," Rose said. "He may be good on horses, but he still don't know when to buy smoked salmon."

They all laughed and Margaret began. "Okay, how about this name, Roger Strong? Rena, I think you had him."

"Cross him off," Rena said. "Too old."

"Okay, next one . . ."

# 21

Professor Guyers looked over the enlightened faces around the large table before him. He had just finished an analysis of *Berg vs. State of Florida*, and since it was already past the hour of dismissal, he stood up.

"Next week then," he said, "I have a real treat for you. *Jamison versus Connought*." He winked. "Do your reading, it's on the handout." He walked over and opened the door to the classroom. Eight of the students in attendance rose, and after collecting their personal things, filed out. Margaret Binton remained seated, watching Guyers carefully.

"I suppose," the teacher said as he turned back, "you have a question to ask me, once again unrelated to ethics?"

"Yes, but this time no dinner prepared. Just a simple question."

He came and sat back down next to her. "Computers again?"

She nodded.

"You know," he said, "it has taken me over twenty years to achieve a tenured position on this law faculty, an equal number of years practicing prior to that in courts around this and other states. I've had numerous articles published in prestigious law journals around the country, not to mention all the years I spent as a student at Harvard Law School, and you persist in seeking my advice in a subject I taught myself in two months two summers ago. I find it very amusing, indeed."

"We seek help where we can," Margaret said. "While I find your knowledge of the law edifying, at this point your knowledge of computers is indispensable."

Professor Guyers sighed and looked at his watch. "How long is this simple question going to take?"

"That all depends," Margaret said. "On how good you are. It's possible you might not even be able to help me."

"Ah, this is to be something of a challenge, then? I like challenges. Difficult law cases as well as difficult puzzles." He leaned back and looked at her out of the corner of his eyes. "Mrs. Binton, do you ever do crossword puzzles?"

She chuckled. "On a bad day," she said, "I take more than an hour with Maleska. I use a pen and have never called for a clue." She looked at him innocently.

"Sounds very similar to my approach," he said. "Perhaps together we could finish one in half an hour. But then, I suppose it's not crosswords you wanted to ask me about, is it?"

"No, I wanted you to find a file in Adrian's computer that doesn't show up on the directory. I assume it's been hidden somehow."

"Ah yes, I remember. Mr. Adrian Lavin, presumedly murdered for something he discovered. Just like in the mystery novels. And how far did you get?"

"I think I know who everyone is, everyone he spoke to and was tracking. . . . I don't know what they did," she hesitated. "I mean all of what they did. Adrian wrote down the innocuous stuff, the material for Divinity Publishing, under the CRCHNOTE file. But I suspect there's other stuff that's more sensitive and I can't find it."

"I don't recall finding anything like that when I looked through."

"Well, I was wondering, maybe there's someplace you didn't look. Some little chip somewhere, some little special hidden place." She looked exasperated. "I don't even have the vocabulary to use to say what I mean. Except that I know the people who build these machines are crafty enough to include some way to hide information. And we have to find where it is."

"Before we get to that, Mrs. Binton," Professor Guyers said, "There's something more important to discuss. What about the ethics here? You're asking me to read private notes. Especially private notes that might have compromising material in them."

"I think we've crossed that bridge already, don't you, Professor?" Margaret said with her simplest smile. "Besides, these are posthumous notes. Adrian Lavin can't be hurt anymore. If anything, he'd want us to search his papers if it meant we could find his murderer. Those are the ethics I see."

"Clearly functional I admit, but not precisely lawful."

"Since when did 'ethical' become synonymous with 'legal'?" Margaret asked.

"Touché"

"Besides, I thought you liked puzzles."

Guyers was silent for a moment. "There is that. . . ." he said finally.

"And if it really bothers you, you don't have to read a thing once we find the information. I will."

"Small consolation," he said. "Like a safecracker arguing that he wasn't the one that grabbed the money. But to be truthful, this does pose some interesting challenges." He shrugged. "I suppose I could give it a try." He looked at Margaret. "For Mr. Lavin's sake."

"For Mr. Lavin's sake," she repeated. "Now, where do we begin? Perhaps in his writing program. That's where he'd keep written data, don't you think?"

"That's the one we already searched," Guyers said.

"Without success. No, if you're right about what we're look-ing for, I think he would be too careful to do that. I think he put them somewhere else, some other program that has noth-ing to do with words. Maybe a game or something." Profes-sor Guyers rubbed the side of his face. "Most games don't permit storing written input, or at least not very much infor-mation, but maybe somewhere else unexpected. Let's check the main directory and see what he has." The law professor turned on the machine and hit a few key strokes. In a mo-ment they found themselves looking at a listing of over thirty programs, each with some shortened title that gave little clue as to what they were. WS5 was the Wordstar word processing program they had already checked, but there was also PRNTMSTR, WINGS, GRPHMKR and dozens more. Profes-sor Guyers shook his head.

"A simple little question, you said. This could take all night."

"Then again, we could get lucky," Margaret said. "Something I very much believe in. I once lost a little sap-phire ring and found it that same night in the building's garbage. In the second bag."

"I don't call that luck, I call that carelessness."

"That's what Oscar said too." She smiled. "But I called it luck because there were twenty more bags to go through. Now, how about if we eliminate some of these programs."

"I wasn't kidding when I said this could take all night. They close this building in an hour," Professor Guyers said.

"Well then, let's go to my apartment. I can offer hot tea, and fresh cookies. And there's no curfew."

Guyers looked at her. "You're an unusually trusting woman, Mrs. Binton. You know little more about me than that I teach a course in law. The law has seen many scoun-drels in its ranks."

"I find," Margaret said, getting up slowly and closing the computer, "that in the very young and the very old, trust is a necessity. Besides, the course you teach is one in ethics. I would hope something has rubbed off."

# 22

In the next three hours Margaret and Guyers went through twenty of the programs, opening and scanning through each one of their associated files, a total of perhaps four hundred operations, and came up with absolutely nothing. They went through World War II air-war games, two versions of Dungeons & Dragons, a graphic program to design banners, greeting and business cards, a check writing and balancing program, and even a program to cross-reference recipes and ingredients with calories and cholesterol counts. But nowhere had Adrian inserted a file, or even a part of a file, which contained the compromising information Margaret was looking for. Margaret was seeing the blue letters of the screen even when she looked away, and they were doing funny things like dancing across her wall or sliding down the refrigerator door. It was clearly time to stop, but they were only five programs away from completion. Guyers held up his cup for a refill of tea, and punched up another program. When he saw the opening menu before him, he realized that NMBRS4 was a Lotus look-alike, a spreadsheet program that enabled the user to design a matrix of numbers with preset relationships, say for a business to compute precisely what the current inventory was worth, or how many days that inventory would last. Since the program dealt mostly in numbers, Guyers decided to move on to another program. But Margaret put her hand on his arm.

"We've looked in all the others, might as well be consistent. Besides, I'm curious why he'd have such a program."

"I'm curious why he had all the other programs too," Guyers said. "Why'd he have the cooking program, or for that matter the program to make greeting cards? I suspect maybe they were free or a friend put them on for him." He shrugged. "Okay, it won't take a minute to look in the NMBRS4 directory." He hit a button and the screen went blank for a moment, and then it showed a list of associated files, ten in all. Margaret leaned closer. She forced her eyes to focus on the small print.

"The first eight files just run the program," Guyers said. "That's what their extensions show."

"But the two others?" Margaret said. The ninth file was called "sales" while the tenth file was titled "Stevenson."

"Uh huh, those are data files."

Margaret sat back for a moment and closed her eyes. As Guyers watched, a small smile spread across her face.

"Yes?" he said.

"I think we've found it. Oh yes, I remember Adrian being quite a wit when he wanted to be. I should have looked for something like this earlier. We could have saved several hours."

"Sales?" the law professor said, but Margaret shook her head.

"Stevenson. Quick, open it up, I'm sure it's there." Guyers punched the command for calling up a file, but instead of a full screen of data, all he got was one line. To be more precise, one character, a question mark. The two of them stared at it for a moment.

"Try it again," Margaret said.

Guyers went through the escape key, and then the normal sequence again and still the question mark appeared.

"I don't think it's asking me what I'm doing, I think it's asking for a special code word. I think Adrian protected this one file with some kind of block. You must be right because it's the only one he did it with." Guyers sat back and frowned.

"No way to find out what the code word is?" Margaret asked. "It's got to be in the machine somewhere."

Guyers shook his head. "If there was a way to find it, it wouldn't be a very good protection program, would it? No, I'm afraid, as some of my students say, we've crashed. And so close too."

There was silence in Margaret's living room for a few moments as Guyers finished off his tea.

"Maybe not," Margaret said finally. "All we need is one word."

"Yes, but I would assume that as a writer, Mr. Lavin had an extensive vocabulary. To find the one word he used would not come under the heading of luck, but rather under the heading of miracle. No, Mrs. Binton, I'm afraid we're at an impasse."

"Try 'shekel'," she said.

"Shekel?"

"Try it. Just humor me."

Guyers hit the keys and almost instantaneously the screen filled with words. He looked at Margaret as his mouth dropped open.

"How . . . ?"

She smiled. "It's the Stevenson file. What, pray tell, did Mr. Robert Louis Stevenson write?"

"Oh, that Stevenson. As I recall, among his works are *Kidnapped, Treasure Island,* let's see . . . *A Child's Garden of Verses.*"

"I think you're forgetting his most famous, *Dr. Jekyll and Mr. Hyde.*"

Guyers's face opened up with the look of divine revelation.

"Ah, as in Mr. Hide."

"Precisely. Adrian's little joke."

"But why shekel and not Jekyll?

"Another little joke. Money was always a concern with him, and shekel was a word I heard him use often. It just made sense, crossword sense. Maleska would have loved it. You didn't see it because you didn't know Adrian."

"That's very generous," Professor Guyers said. "Now, let's see what we have unlocked. I can see that this program allows not only for the insertion of numbers, but also of words, perhaps for headings. It looks like he used them as little minifiles, one for each person." He bent closer.

Margaret put her hand on his arm. "You needn't continue, you know. As you said, there are some legitimate reservations for a professor of ethics rooting around in someone else's personal material. Besides, it's late." She looked at her watch. "Past midnight, in fact."

Guyers looked at her without flinching. "Mrs. Binton, I've come this far, I'm not about to back off at the moment of success. Besides, I can't remember when I've had such fun. Maybe when I tried a case before the Supreme Court. And, as I recall mentioning in one of my earlier lectures, many ethical questions are matters of interpretation. In this case I tend to agree with your interpretation. I can see no harm in my assisting you." He smiled tiredly.

"In that case, I want to get something straight. My name is Margaret. Mrs. Binton was someone married to a Mr. Binton who passed away a long time ago."

"And my name's William," the professor said simply. "Now, shall we continue?"

"Certainly," Margaret said. "I'll put on another pot of tea."

In another hour and a half they had read everything. Guyers had been making notes, and when he finally shut down the computer, he also put his pen down. Margaret was sitting on the couch, a decidedly perplexed look on her face.

"More than you anticipated?" he asked her.

"Not so much the quantity," she replied, "but the detail. Where did he get some of that information? An alcoholic pilot, a crossdressing lawyer with a prestigious firm, someone else hiding a case of AIDS, a high school athlete taking steroids, a well-to-do wife who doubles as an afternoon call girl." She shook her head. "Someone else who no one suspects is on methadone. It's just not the kind of information people are apt to divulge, even anonymously. Adrian was persuasive, but not quite that much. No one is."

"You think he made it up?"

"No, I think it's all genuine. I think he was collecting these stories for use somewhere else." She hesitated for a minute. "William, let's look in the other file, the one marked 'sales.'" He hit a few more keys and this time, the new file opened up without a code word. They both bent over the computer and read silently. After a minute Margaret looked up.

"Here it is," she said softly. "A proposal and a tentative outline for a book called *Saintly Fun*. No doubt all to be submitted somewhere after his final payment from Divinity Publishing. That's where all this other material was going. And, no doubt, the money from *A St. Martin's Centennial* was going to support him while he wrote his steamy blockbuster. He had it all planned out." She sat back in her chair. "But the question remains, how did he find all the stories? I'm convinced they're all true. I recognize a few of them already."

Guyers rubbed the bridge of his nose and closed his eyes. He was tired, and it was way past his bedtime.

"Margaret," he said. "I'm afraid I'm not going to be much help at this late hour. I need some rest. Besides," he smiled thinly, "sometimes the most creative solutions come in dreams."

"Yes, I suppose," she said, then hesitated for a moment.

"You're welcome to stay here, William. There's this couch . . ."

"Thank you," he said, "but us old bachelors have our peculiarities. I, for one, like to sleep in my own bed." He got up and walked to the door. "I'll Xerox these notes and bring back a copy tomorrow if you like, say at six o'clock?"

"That would be a big help," Margaret said. "Then you can meet some of my other friends. I think you'd enjoy them."

"If they're like you, I'm sure I will."

# 23

Renzuli looked at the two detectives seated before him. He liked to have the people in his office seated, respectful. Besides, when he got up to make a point, they had to look up. Renzuli was sensitive about his height, and even more sensitive now because one of the detectives before him was Laura Green, pushing six feet. Sniff crossed her legs, and the tight skirt hiked up a few inches on her calves. Renzuli made an effort and looked at her partner, Detective Edwards, a man whose five o'clock shadow appeared at high noon and lengthened during the rest of the day.

"So Melendez has finally sobered?" he asked. "With no alibi for the night Lavin was killed?"

Scratch nodded. "And his knife had the kind of blade that could have made Lavin's wound."

"Good." Renzuli smiled. "What's his story?"

"Denies everything," Edwards continued. "Says he found the wallet in the park the day after the killing. He was alone, no one saw him pick it up. Sounds phony to me. Just his set of fingerprints on the wallet."

"I wish Lavin's had also been on there," Sniff broke in.

"And why's that?" Renzuli asked, bringing his attention back to her.

"Lavin's wallet should have his prints, no? Without them means the wallet could have been wiped clean. Why would Melendez wipe the wallet, then put his prints on?"

"You don't think Melendez is it?" Renzuli asked, and stood up.

"I just look at the facts," Green said. "Maybe he is, maybe he isn't."

"Yeah, well right now he's all we've got," Renzuli said.

"Besides," Edwards said, "a guy is wearing a wallet in his back pocket, he sits down, he stands up, the wallet is wiped clean a dozen times a day."

Sniff shrugged.

"Any positive ID yet?" The lieutenant asked.

"We've tried," she answered. "We've canvassed the entire neighborhood, but no one's willing to go on record Melendez was on the block. And the Evarts woman who gave us the description of the guy running after the murder says maybe, but can't be more definite. I don't think it's enough to go to the DA with."

Renzuli paced behind his desk. "Damn," he said. "Here we got this son of a bitch with the victim's wallet, credit cards and all, and we can't tie him up. Guy's got a record a mile long, even." He turned and glowered at his two detectives. "Find something," he said. "Or threaten the son of a bitch until he breaks."

"Unless he's not the real murderer," Sniff said.

Renzuli glowered at her. "This is some goddamn department. Lots of support here." He sat back down and nodded towards the door. "Unless you got something else of interest, you can let yourselves out." He bent down to some papers on his desk as the two detectives got up. When they were outside, Green shook her head.

"I think you're wrong on this one, Sonny. I have this feeling we got one unlucky dude in Melendez."

"Yeah, maybe, but when I'm finished with him he's going to be a lot more unlucky."

"That's what I like about you," Sniff said. "You're so open-minded."

"Hey, don't knock success," Scratch said, and the two of them went up the staircase to their desks.

# 24

A ll right, so here it is," Margaret said, looking down at her notes. "We know who all of the people in Adrian's Stevenson file are. Picasso is the bully, steroid taker; Checkmate is the lawyer and cross-dresser, Evergreen is Nancy Sherwin, the woman with too much money, and a very active social, or should I say, *professional* life. Wrench is the Lothario in Mrs. Edelston's building with AIDS, Airhead is a pilot with a taste for liquid refreshment, and Statue is the dancer on methadone. God, what a nightmare. Then there's Morpenzo the alien and Tyler, the drug-dealing artist."

"I'm impressed," Professor Guyers said. "Quite a handle you have on this." The other people in Margaret's apartment looked around at him but said nothing. He had been introduced to them ten minutes earlier, but had sat quietly off to the side, watching them. For this meeting he had worn his best three-piece lawyerly pinstripe suit, a choice that looked as out of place as a tuxedo in a convention of taxi drivers.

"Well, we are taking this very seriously," Berdie finally assured the professor, eying his neat suit.

"I have no doubt of that," Professor Guyers smiled back at her politely.

There was an awkward silence for a moment.

"Well, he could have been blackmailing any one of them," Pancher interrupted. "If his information was correct."

Margaret shook her head. "I don't think so. I knew Adrian. He just wasn't the type to blackmail."

"You want us to believe that he didn't try a little free-lance extortion," Durso asked incredulously, "just because you have a good feeling about him, Margaret? People aren't like that. People tend to follow their economic interests right down to the letter."

"Amen, Dr. Marx," Roosa said, and chuckled.

Durso knocked his pipe on the edge of an ashtray and stuck it back in his mouth. "Every time there's money to be made in this capitalistic mecca of greed we call America, people jump at the opportunity."

"Give it a rest," Roosa added. "Every time you open your mouth you sound like a Russian textbook from the thirties."

Durso reddened, but Margaret held up her hand. "Please." She looked sternly at Roosa and Durso. "Let's not give Professor Guyers the wrong impression here. We are all supposed to be working together." She waited a long moment before continuing. "Now, if Adrian was extorting money it certainly didn't show up in his apartment. The only expensive thing he had was his computer and that came from his advance from Divinity. No, he wasn't threatening anyone. . . . at least not on purpose. I think someone found out he had some compromising information about them, something obviously they themselves had not divulged, and they got scared. They couldn't be sure Adrian was going to be quite so honorable."

She looked again around the circle of friends in her

living room, especially Durso. "But that's something we can find out," she continued. "We can ask the people in the Stevenson file whether Adrian put any pressure on them. Even if one of them is the murderer and denies it, we'll have all the other responses. I think you'll find I'm right. I don't see Adrian as a blackmailer. So, it's quite clear to me, what we have to do is go back and question the people in this file. Those are the people with the most to lose."

"So divide the names," Berdie said. "We can do this all tomorrow. I think Sidney already had the Sherwin woman. He should go back . . ."

"And I could take Mr. Tyler again," Pancher said.

Five minutes later they were finished with the assignments and people were on their way out. Margaret went to clean up. Sid patted Guyers on the shoulder as he went by.

"Nice meeting you, Professor. I hope she's doing well in your class because I can't wait to see Margaret in a three-piece suit, just like yours." Guyers smiled awkwardly as the others followed Sid towards the front door. The law professor waited until the last one had left, then found Margaret washing glasses in the kitchen.

"Mind if I come tomorrow night again? I must admit, this is becoming somewhat compelling."

Margaret looked at him. "Only if you do me one favor. Try and find something to wear that's a little more . . . casual. Maybe something in a sweatshirt look."

"Margaret, I've never owned a sweatshirt in my life," the professor said.

"If I'm not mistaken, they sell them in the bookstore," she added. "I think you'll find they're quite comfortable." She walked with him to the door. "Tomorrow then, same time."

"Same time," he agreed. "And don't forget to do your reading. We don't want to overlook our ethics class, do we?"

"Of course not," Margaret grinned. "Life does go on."

# 25

"Yes?"

The thin, willowy figure of Dena Duvall was over-shadowed by the blimp that was Rose Gaffery standing in her doorway. It was early the next morning and Rose, having rotated her best sweater up to the outside layer, had just arrived to ask Ms. Duval some questions. As shy as she was about meeting new people, she was not about to let all her friends down.

"My name is Rose Gaffery, Miss Duvall. Could I ask you a favor?"

"How'd you get in?" the other woman asked. "I mean downstairs?"

"Oh, that." Rose smiled. "Mrs. Edelston from upstairs knows a friend of mine, Mrs. Bernstein. The two of them talk about opera all the time."

The other woman shook her head, but seemed to relax somewhat. She inspected the large woman in front of her now more closely, but Rose had done a good job getting ready. Besides the bright yellow acrylic sweater, she had put on her best pair of sneakers, worn the clean Harvard sweatpants, and had spent twenty minutes combing her hair. This was respectability. She had even parked all of her shopping bags downstairs with Roosa, who promised to watch them faithfully.

"A favor?" the younger woman repeated. "What favor?"

"I understand you're in the methadone program, and I was wondering if you could just tell me how to get started. This other friend of mine . . ."

The expression on the young dancer's face went ashen. Her body stiffened as though she were posing for a still life, and then she let out the breath she had trapped inside.

"Methadone?" she said noncommittally, but her face told the truth. Her eyes grew small and bore into Rose's face.

"Yes. You know, it's not easy to get into a program like you . . ." Rose continued.

"How . . . ?" the other woman started, then stopped herself. She hesitated for a moment, looked to both sides in the hallway, then took a step back. "Come in for a moment," she said.

Rose took a step inside, and the door closed behind her with a bang. The dancer paced into the living room, rubbing her hands together, then turned around.

"How the hell did you find out? The program guaranteed me absolute secrecy. I've told no one." She rubbed behind her neck with one hand. "This could absolutely ruin my career if it gets out. No one wants a reformed junkie in their corps de ballet, especially Sabo Haruki." She was quite besides herself.

"I don't know about no corpse of ballet," Rose said. "All I know is my friend needs help. And Adrian said . . ."

"Lavin!" The other woman almost screamed. "That pesky writer. I never told him a goddamn thing about that. Other things maybe, but never about that."

"Maybe he talked to some of your friends." Rose squinted at her and shook her head. "Lady, I'm sorry if I got you all upset. I thought you didn't care who knew. Adrian didn't say nothing about it being a secret. Truth is, seeing as how shook up you are, I'm surprised he didn't try to, well, maybe get some money out of you—I mean to keep quiet about it."

"I would have paid it," she said angrily, then started to cry softly. Rose waited patiently until the other woman started speaking again.

"It's just so hard to kick old habits," the younger woman said. "Things you get into in bad times. And now I'm just getting somewhere." She took a deep breath, and Rose took a step closer and patted her shoulder.

"There, I know how you feel. We all need some help sometimes. You don't have to worry about me, though. I won't tell anyone."

"I would have paid him," Dena repeated. "But he never asked. I didn't know he knew."

"Well, Adrian had his ways, I guess. It's really nothing to be ashamed of. Lots of people on methadone."

"Not with Sabo Haruki's group. He demands pure bodies. It's his gospel." She looked down at Rose, who was still touching her shoulder. "We were going on tour this summer. I don't take that much. I was hoping I could be off it by then."

"Maybe you will be."

"Maybe." The dancer took a step back and shook her head in a gesture that was meant to erase all her troubled thoughts. "You really won't tell?"

"What's to tell?" Rose smiled. "And if you're so worried, I suppose I can always find someone else to ask. Maybe even just call up Social Services. It just seemed better to get the information from someone that's been through it."

The other woman nodded, hesitated, then turned slowly and wrote something down on a piece of paper. She ripped the sheet off the pad and handed it back to Rose.

"This program didn't tell, I'm sure. I can't believe it. No one knew."

Rose shrugged. "Adrian found out somehow," she said.

"Mr. Lavin was a very persuasive man," Dena said coldly. "And now I see, very dangerous."

Rose nodded, then opened the door. "Thanks for the help. You know, I've seen a lot of people on the streets and I can tell you got your problem beat. You'll let Mrs. Edelston know when you're gonna dance next. I'd like to go see you. I bet you're good."

The dancer smiled. "I could call you."

"Afraid not. My phone's out of order. The coin return is stuffed with chewing gum." She smiled and trundled out of the dancer's apartment, heading quickly downstairs to retrieve her shopping bags before Roosa got the notion to look inside them. "Can't trust anyone these days," she muttered, and started rearranging her sweaters with the cleanest one now on the inside.

Durso found Picasso, a.k.a. Edward Hobson, hanging out on the stoop in front of his apartment. He had spoken to Hobson before, briefly confirming that Hobson had been one of Adrian's subjects. Nothing had been mentioned about his "punch-out" games on the subway platforms. Durso had just found out that he was in the habit of going to St. Martin's Church with his mother, and that Adrian had interviewed him a few times. That was before the Stevenson file showed him to also be a steroid user. Now that Durso took a moment to study him, he could clearly see that below the fresh, black, youthful face, Hobson was a physical brute. His arms looked like sculpted challah bread and his neck was the size of a telephone pole. Intimidating, Durso thought, especially to someone like himself who had never been a particularly good or interested athlete. As a child, Durso had spent all of his time indoors studying books to become a teacher. Athletics were the last hope for the mentally impaired to support themselves and not be a burden on their family. Of course, all that had changed, and now it was the athletes who made all the money, and the teachers who were mentally impaired. Why

126

else go into such a dangerous, underpaid, and unrewarding career? But back then . . .

"What 'choo want?" the mass of flesh and muscle asked as Durso sat down next to him.

"Hello Edward, remember me? Couple of days ago I asked about Adrian."

"Yeah, I remember," he said lazily.

Durso pulled his old cherry pipe out of his pocket with one hand and with the other, a book of matches. In one practiced motion he lit what little tobacco remained inside and started puffing.

"Filthy habit if you be asking me," Hobson said, giving the older man a sideways glance. "Don't 'choo know smoke ain't no good for you?"

"Us old-timers find it hard to give up our habits." Durso smiled. "Besides, I dare say it's not as bad a habit as, say, listening to rap music." There was silence on the bench for a moment as Durso puffed up a small cloud. "Or, for that matter, as taking steroids."

Hobson leaned back and looked carefully at the older man's neck.

"What 'choo know about steroids, pop?" There was a little edge to his voice.

"What I read. Another little vice of mine. Ben Johnson in the Olympics, and all that."

The young man seemed to relax. He even managed a smile.

"Yeah, a real shame."

"I think," Durso continued slowly, "that what you consider a shame differs significantly from my conception."

"What 'choo mean?"

"I think the shame for you is that he got caught."

Hobson's smile faded just as quickly as it had appeared.

"Be careful what you be saying, old man. If you don't want no trouble."

Durso shook his head. "I'm not the one who's going to

be in trouble, Edward. I'm not the one taking steroids."
Durso puffed softly on his pipe.

"Damn!" Hobson exclaimed and leaned closer. His
young face looked both defiant and nervous at the same time.
His hand, which was approximately the size of a frying pan,
curled into a tight, hard fist. Durso remembered the game of
"punch-out" Edward and his friends played, one punch for
a knockout to win the pool of money. He had no doubt that
all their victims were far more innocent than he was at this
particular moment. "I'm not here, Edward, to threaten you,"
Durso continued quickly. "I'm just an old man with a question or two. This is just between the two of us. No one's going
to get hurt."

"How you know that, old man. How you know I won't
flatten you right now?"

"You'd have to flatten them also, since they've been
watching us the whole time." He pointed across the street to
where Sid and Pancher and Margaret were sitting on three
separate stoops, waiting. "Now you probably could, but not
before there was a lot of shouting. And three witnesses,"
Durso shook his head, "hard to beat. You wouldn't want that,
especially since you're one of Marcus Garvey High School's
best basketball players. Just like you wouldn't want them to
know about the games you and your friends play on the
subway platforms."

A clouded look came over Edward's face, and slowly,
very slowly, his fist unfurled. "Damn, Adrian told you about
the 'punch-out'? He said he wouldn't say anything. . . . the
dude promised."

"He kept his word. But he kept some notes that I read.
Actually, what he wrote indicated that you had only been
involved once."

"Yeah. I wasn't going out with them again. Bunch of
niggers with too much time on their hands and nowhere to
go."

"Not like an up-and-coming basketball star." Durso
leaned closer. "But you know what, taking steroids was just

as foolish. They don't like them in high school, and in college they'll throw you out and take away any scholarship you might get."

Hobson looked at him through narrowed eyes for a full minute before saying anything. Finally he asked, "How you know about the steroids? I never told nothing to Adrian about them."

"He knew. He had it in his notes. You sure you didn't maybe slip and mention it once?"

"No man. That other stuff, the 'punch-out,' hey, around school, everyone's doing that. The brothers read about 'wilding' and figured, hey, look what we're missing. If someone found out I maybe would have gotten in trouble, but nothing I couldn't talk my way out of. With steroids man, the coach told people they'd be dropped."

"And you continued?"

The young boy shrugged. "Lotta people be doin' them around the gym. Besides," he flexed the muscle in his arm and the flesh jumped into a knot as thick as a hawser on the QE2, "I liked what it did for my body. So did the girls."

Durso thought for a moment. "And Adrian never . . . threatened you with telling? Tried to get money from you?"

"I told you, man, I was very careful. I have no idea how he found out." He shook his head. "No, he never threatened me. I thought he was okay."

"I see." Durso rubbed his chin. After a moment he pulled his feet closer to get up.

"Tell me something," Hobson said. "How come you so interested? Guy was mugged, right?"

"Yeah, mugged," the retired schoolteacher said, and stood up. "Thanks, Edward. You be careful now. And if you want some free advice, lay off the steroids. The best place for you is on a basketball court, not a gym." He stuck his pipe back in his mouth, and walked across the street to his friends. The four of them converged, walked together to the end of the block and turned out of sight on Broadway. Edward Hobson watched them go with a confused expression on his face. One

129

thing he figured, maybe it was time to cool it a little with the steroids. He'd need a new prescription soon anyway, and the little Ecuadorian doctor who was writing them for him was showing signs of pulling back. Yeah, maybe now was the time. Before he got into more trouble.

Peter Sherill looked like Adolphe Menjou without the mustache. At least that's what Rena thought the moment he opened the door for her. Medium-sized man with a round face, dark hair and eyes that expressed more charm than was called for, as though they were on audition.

"Excuse me, Mr. Sherill, my name is Rena Bernstein, and I was just having a pleasant chat with my friend Mrs. Edelston down on the second floor, when she mentioned your name. She's really quite a busybody, you know, but every now and then she has a good idea." Sherill forced a smile but remained noncommittal.

"What idea was it that she had?" he said. "If you are looking for a donation for Red Cross or something, I've already given."

"I'm sure you have," Rena said politely. "A man in your condition."

"Excuse me?" he said, but there was a flicker of nervousness behind his eyes, and they ceased being quite so charming.

"Well, you know, someone who's tested HIV positive might be more inclined to donate to a medical charity, say, than to one for Haitian boat people."

Sherill looked down at this slight older woman wearing a plain green polyester dress and sneakers, topped by an orange felt beret, and grabbed on to the door frame.

"What did you say?"

"Actually, that's what I wanted to ask you about. I know there are a lot of AIDS patients in the neighborhood, and I was wondering if you thought it would be a good idea to start a volunteer service where some of us old-timers came in to help with little chores. You know, laundry and shopping and things like that. I mean later on when it gets harder for you to do it yourself." She smiled innocently and took a step forward. "You mind if I come in? Maybe we can sit and chat about it for a moment."

Absently, Sherill took a step backwards and watched as Rena walked through to the living room and sat down. His face was ashen.

"You know, everyone thinks us old-timers are a big nuisance, but I said that it's not true, that we could perform a service that's sorely needed. Don't you agree?"

Sherill had walked over and was now sitting in a chair in front of her. He leaned his trim frame closer, put his face no further than eight inches away from Rena's, and said in a somewhat shaky voice, "Why do you think I tested positive for AIDS?"

"Oh, why Mr. Lavin told me."

"He couldn't have," Sherill said. "I never told him anything of the kind."

"But he knew," Rena persisted. "Whether you told him or not. Don't you think it's better dealing with it openly?" Her voice had lost much of its innocence.

"Better for who?" Sherill said, raising his voice. "You know how people with AIDS are treated, like pariahs!" He got up and walked to the door. "I don't need any concern or moralizing from some old lady," he said. "I'll thank you to keep your nose out of my affairs. And as far as your idea is concerned, when and if I need help, I'll find it. And not from a bunch of people who need walkers and wheelchairs themselves."

Rena shook her head sadly and stood up. As she passed him on the way to the door, she stopped and turned to face him.

"I don't understand why you find this such a threat," she said. "I just want to help."

"A hundred-percent fatality rate is very threatening," Sherill said sarcastically.

"Unless someone else has," she continued. "I mean,

threatened you. Perhaps Mr. Lavin? I'm sure people in your condition are very vulnerable to that sort of thing."

"I told you, how could he threaten me? He didn't know. Now, I'm a busy man. Tell Mrs. Edelston that there's a lot more to life than gossip." He held the door for Rena and watched as she walked out.

Checkmate was Templeton Winterspoon Jr., and he lived in one of the nicest apartments on Central Park West. Being one of the partners in a prestigious law firm like White, Horvath, and Mead certainly gave one benefits most regular working people never saw. In the case of Winterspoon, he had a front apartment on a high floor, a full-time cook, a daughter who just graduated from Princeton, and a wardrobe of suits that would have made Oscar de la Renta jealous. With all that, it was understandable that Templeton Winterspoon Jr. was polite; so polite, in fact, that he actually offered Margaret Binton a drink when she came that afternoon at 5:00. Margaret had already telephoned and gotten his permission to discuss their mutual friend, Mr. Lavin. He offered her the drink because he was standing there holding one of his own when she rang the bell. Besides, he knew about older women; they all liked their afternoon sherry.

"Yes, thank you," Margaret said as she sat down in one of his comfortable sofas, "I'll have a Jack Daniel's on the rocks, twist of lemon."

"You came about Mr. Lavin?" Winterspoon asked after he handed her the drink a few moments later. "We spent some hours chatting about things but I never suspected that he'd have such a horrible accident."

"It wasn't an accident," Margaret said softly as she sipped her drink.

"Yes. That's true."

"Of course, one could have foreseen, since Adrian was compiling a lot of sensitive information, it might have, shall we say, backfired on him."

"Sensitive information?" The lawyer looked at her innocently. "We never talked about really private matters, just mostly about innocuous things. What my family was like, our church activities, the kind of work I do at White, Horvath, and Mead. He told me he was doing a study of the people who went to St. Martin's Church and merely wanted to get a profile of their parishioners, how the church has helped them." Winterspoon took a long sip and finished the drink he was holding. He put it down on a nearby table and folded his hands.

"Is that why, Mr. Winterspoon, he noted that you were still suffering from your divorce, were having a problem with alcohol, and had a daughter that was about to leave school to get married to someone you found totally unacceptable? Merely innocuous things?"

Winterspoon's eyes opened wide, and so did his mouth in a forced smile. The total effect was something like a clown greeting a two year old.

"Well, maybe some more private things did slip out. I had to let my cook go when I found out that Adrian was also interviewing her when I was at the office. But those things were certainly innocent enough when viewed in the light of what happened to Mr. Lavin." He looked back down at the empty glass and then decided that this was shaping up into a two-drink discussion. He got up, refreshed the glass, and came back.

"True enough," Margaret said when he had rejoined her. She took another sip of her bourbon, smiled as she felt its warmth down her throat, and proceeded. "But perhaps there were other things Adrian knew about that were more, shall we say, compromising, especially for a man in your position."

Templeton Witherspoon Jr. smiled indulgently. "Don't let your imagination get carried away with you, Mrs. Binton. You may have been a friend of Mr. Lavin's, but looking for ghosts in empty closets is not going to do anyone any good. I wasn't aware that Mr. Lavin knew about my daughter's childish intentions, or about some of the other things, but I

133

can assure you that's all he knew about. We lead quiet lives here. There wasn't anything else to know."

Margaret looked at him closely, then reached into her handbag. "Mind if I smoke?" she asked.

"If you plan to be here that long, go ahead," he said.

Margaret scribbled down the number of the cigarette, wrapped the pack back up, and lit it quickly. She looked back up at the middle-aged lawyer.

"This is a little awkward for me, Mr. Winterspoon. In my old age, one thing I've learned is that everyone has quirks and idiosyncrasies, and as long as they don't hurt anyone, then we should all be tolerant. Quirks are what make people interesting, don't you think?" She shifted uncomfortably in her seat. "So you'll understand that what I have to say now implies no judgment on my part. I'm only reporting facts as I was given them." She took a puff on her cigarette, and a cloud of smoke swirled up to the high ceiling.

"Could you be less mysterious, madam? Are we talking about my idiosyncrasy of having oysters at McGann's two days a week for lunch?"

"We are not, sir," Margaret said and leaned forward. "We are talking about your habit of wearing panty hose under your three-piece suit pants. Probably quite as often." She blushed a color of pale cedar and swallowed the last of her bourbon. "That is what we are talking about."

The effect on Templeton Witherspoon Jr. was immediate. He jumped out of his seat, glowered down at the woman in front of him, reached for his glass awkwardly, spilling half of its contents on the rug, then slowly, sat back down.

"Perhaps that is also why you fired your cook, Mr. Witherspoon, for telling Adrian about some of your favorite fashion accessories. What is it they call it. . . . cross-dressing? I for one can't understand why anyone who didn't have to would want to wear all those uncomfortable things anyway: girdles, brassieres, *bustiers,* teddies." Margaret took a breath. "I suppose you had them all?"

Winterspoon was shaking his head slowly. He seemed

truly amazed. For over a minute he said nothing, just moved his head from side to side.

"It's a lie," he said finally.

"Mr. Winterspoon, I assure you I am not the kind of woman that goes around suggesting to every person I meet that they are engaged in some peculiar behavior like cross-dressing. I found out about your particular fetish through Mr. Lavin's notes. How he got the information is another matter."

Winterspoon sat quite still, only his head moving slowly. "I don't understand. . . . he never mentioned anything to me."

"No threats?" Margaret asked.

"No." The lawyer looked dumbfounded. "How did he . . . ?"

"Perhaps a laundress?"

The well-groomed man seemed to refocus. His eyes narrowed and he stopped his head from wagging. "I thought I was being very careful." He got up finally and paced to a window and returned. "I even did my own laundry for those things." He looked down at her. "You won't say anything, will you? I can't tell you how embarrassing it would be if some of the other partners . . ."

"I am not here to threaten you, Mr. Winterspoon. Just to find out some facts. As I said, at my age you've seen just about everything," she smiled, ". . . well, perhaps not quite everything."

He smiled then, for the first time, and sat back down. He looked at her friendly, lined face. There was silence in the room for another minute, then he started speaking.

"It was just a joke at first. One night when my wife had gone out once again to her bridge game, I put on her hosiery. I don't know why, it was there and I was all alone. Then I put on her lipstick and rouge and spent the evening watching sitcoms. You can't imagine how your perspective shifts when you watch 'Cheers' in drag." He chuckled. "When she returned I was back to being Mr. Winterspoon Jr. again. Of course it was so excruciatingly depraved that I couldn't wait for her bridge nights. But I didn't abuse it and always stayed at home. I was too afraid to go out." He took a deep breath. "Then we started having problems—actually we'd had problems for years—but they got more serious when my daughter was at Princeton. No one home but the two of us. Maybe that's why she was going out with her friends so much. Anyway, one thing led to another and she just left. One day about two years ago she said she had had enough, that was it. It had nothing to do with the cross-dressing, I can assure you; she'd never seen me like that. After twenty-five years, she just walked out. I didn't feel guilty, just empty. I tried finding a way out of my depression through alcohol, but it only helped at night. I couldn't come in to work soused. I needed something for the daytime, and that's when I thought of . . . putting things on under the suits."

"And did it work?" Margaret asked softly.

He nodded. "Once I got over the amazement at what I was doing, it worked well. You can't imagine how exciting it is to be in the boardroom of a multinational corporation discussing a takeover strategy with five CEO sharks dressed in sheer taupe panty hose and a Maidenform underneath my Turnbill and Asser broadcloth shirts. Delicious." He leaned back and actually laughed. "I was positively radiant."

"Are you homosexual, Mr. Winterspoon?" Margaret asked.

He leaned forward again quickly. "Of course not," he said with a frown. "This was just a kind of entertainment. A way to get over a difficult period in my life. I can assure you I'm still interested in the opposite sex. And the last thing I'd want to be is an exhibitionist. You must understand that this was all very . . . private. That's why I don't understand how in earth you found out."

Margaret took another puff of her cigarette, then put it out in a nearby crystal ashtray. The Jack Daniel's had gone right down on an empty stomach, and she was feeling the need for a bathroom.

"Not to worry," she said with a smile and stood up slowly. She steadied herself on the back of her chair, and faced him. "Unless, of course, you killed him."

"Me?" The lawyer sounded aghast. "That's absurd. Why on earth should I?"

"Maybe he was blackmailing you?"

"That's a laugh. Adrian? That's a bit like suggesting Woody Allen do a 'Rambo' film. One of the reasons I allowed him in and chatted with him openly was that he was so well-mannered, so cultured. Blackmail . . . out of the question."

"I suppose," Margaret shrugged. "You certainly don't fit the description of the man seen running away. Do you mind if I use your bathroom?"

"Go ahead." Witherspoon pointed. "First door on the left."

"Well, it's been very enlightening," Margaret said, and started herself off somewhat shakily in the direction he had indicated. "Oh, in case you're interested," she said casually, "I just read they're having a special on L'eggs at Woolworth's. One forty-nine. Limited supplies."

"Thank you, but I buy everything at my local pharmacy," Witherspoon said icily, and watched as she disappeared inside the bathroom. A minute later she emerged and headed towards the entrance door. "Good day, Mrs. Binton," he said, pulling open the door in front of her. "I trust you'll keep our little secret to yourself."

"Me? But of course, I'm a paragon of discretion," she said, "an absolute paragon."

Sid was wearing his cleanest shirt and his best tie, but the look he was getting from Nancy Sherwin said it was still not enough. Perhaps it was the black-and-white houndstooth jacket that caused her to raise an eyebrow when she opened the door on him. Somehow the pattern did not go well with a striped shirt, or for that matter with the wide tie with beige polka dots he had purchased specially for a 1940 Harry James concert. He remained fixed in the doorway under her gaze like a butterfly pinned to cardboard, waiting. Dominick, the doorman from downstairs, had sent him up after laying the groundwork, but so far she was making no moves to let him in.

Sid repeated his last question. "May I come in? It's about Mr. Lavin."

She gave him a final glance, from head to scuffed toe, and shrugged.

"I don't usually entertain strange men in my apartment," she began, "but I suppose I can make an exception. Dominick said you were harmless." She stepped back and swirled into her apartment. Sid started after her, led by her eighty-dollar-an-ounce scent. They passed out of the foyer, through a large living room with a grand piano, and into a small sitting room lined with books. Mrs. Sherwin sat down behind an ornate desk with gilded edges and offered Sid a seat on something that looked French. At least it was upholstered in silk, that much he knew. Silk to match the silk Mrs. Sherwin was wearing in her expensive lounging outfit. Relaxed on the chair, she reminded Sid of Jean Harlow in *Hell's Angels*.

"This will have to be somewhat short," she said. "My husband will be back soon and he likes me to be attentive. What about Mr. Lavin?"

"I see." Sid rubbed his chin. "Well, I guess I should get right to the heart of things. As you know, Mrs. Sherwin, Mr. Lavin was doing a book on the church. You were one of his subjects."

"Yes," she said, "and I was flattered. But I told him I didn't know why he chose me. I'd say I lead a rather boring life compared to some of the other people that go there. I mean, Roger and I are wealthy, certainly, but old money is usually boring money, if you know what I mean."

"Oh, he found some interesting things to put down." Sid smiled with enough exaggeration to get on Mrs. Sherwin's nerves.

"Yes?" She raised her eyebrows. "Like what? That trash that was in the *Post* about the golf pro? Pure lies."

"No, from what I understand, Mr. Lavin usually stayed away from recycled hearsay. He liked to uncover his own information. That's why he was particularly interested in your arrangements." He watched as her eyes grew small and angry. "I'm sorry, Mrs. Sherwin," he continued, "no reason to be confusing here. Lavin knew that you were operating a kind of free-lance prostitution business here. He found it interesting that a lady in your standing should be so . . . employed." Sid smiled thinly. "I don't, but I'm older than he was and am consequently more charitable."

Mrs. Sherwin looked Sid up and down trying to size up the opposition. She must have concluded that this was more in the nature of pest than threat, and leaned back in her chair. Her eyes softened and her face took on a sardonic grin.

"Thank you. I'm sure I appreciate your tolerance. And how, pray tell, do you think Adrian arrived at such a peculiar conviction?"

"I can only guess," Sid said, "but of course you could enlighten me. I take it you never told him directly?"

"You must be kidding, old man. Either that or you take me for the biggest fool north of Sardi's. If I were . . . employed, as you suggest, I certainly wouldn't confirm it to a total stranger." Her smile enlarged. "I'm not even sure I'd confirm it to a close friend, either. So let's just say you will have to remain unenlightened, no matter how intriguing I find this conversation. And make no mistake, I do find it intriguing. Life can be so boring sometimes that even the most outrageous ideas can be interesting." She stretched on the chair like a bored cat. With the movement her silk peignoir opened slightly at the top, exposing just enough décolletage to grab Sid's attention for a moment. Nancy Sherwin looked entirely satisfied.

"Outrageous ideas usually get one into trouble," Sid

said, and shifted on his chair. "And trouble is never 'intriguing,' as you put it."

"To some people," Nancy Sherwin said, and looked at her nails.

"Perhaps your husband is one of them?" Sid said lightly.

The other woman looked up quickly and her eyes narrowed once again. She straightened up and leaned forward, all illusion of languor disappearing in her new posture. "Mr. Rossman," she said, "this is starting to sound like a threat. I'm surprised. Dominick said you were harmless."

"Quite harmless, I assure you. Information is what I'm after, nothing more. Your relationship with your husband is your own business. Your relationship with Adrian, however, is what I find intriguing." He paused. "Did he ever threaten you with what information he had?"

"Of course not. If he had, do you think I would have continued to allow him in? Assuming, for the moment, that he had any information. I found him amusing, that was all, and bright, and sometimes my afternoons could drag on so. You understand. One can't go running to country clubs in the rain, or take long lunches every day. It plays havoc with one's figure." She stood up. "No, he never threatened me. In fact I fancy he enjoyed coming to see me just to talk. And now I think our little talk is about to end."

"And that's all it was?"

"That's all."

Sid stood up also. "I'm sure you can be very entertaining when you try." He nodded slightly and started retracing his steps to the front door.

She followed slowly behind him but paused in the middle of the foyer. "Can I ask you what reason you have to be so interested in Mr. Lavin? You didn't say you were from the police."

"Purely in the realm of neighborhood safety," Sid said.

"Neighborhood safety," she repeated with a chuckle. "I like that. I feel safer already knowing you're out there. Good day, Mr. Rossman. I hope you find out what you're looking for.''

"So do I," Sid answered, and turned to go.

Roosa found the pilot at home when he came to deliver the flowers. One thing he knew, no one ever turns down a mysterious bouquet of flowers until reading the card. Lee Matson was no different. He opened the door and was waiting for Roosa at the end of the corridor on the third-floor landing. The building did not have a doorman, but it did have a marble foyer, an electronic intercom with a camera, and a mirrored self-service elevator. As New York real estate went, it was a comfortable building, but not extravagant. Lee Matson was a man in his early forties, old enough to have an established career, but young enough to still have a bank account in low figures. Like the building, not extravagant. He looked trim in a white polo shirt and a pair of gray cotton slacks and penny loafers. In contrast, Roosa was wearing his Midas-muffler baseball cap and a windbreaker that was at least one size too small. His glasses were down on his nose, because the electrician's tape holding on the earpieces provided little tension. But the bouquet was real, a six-dollar expense Roosa had sprung for just to gain entry. Now, as he exited the elevator to meet the other man, he could see the mixture of curiosity and skepticism on Matson's face.

"They got a card?" the pilot asked as Roosa reached him.

"They're from Adrian Lavin," the older man said tiredly, and handed them to him. They were the ubiquitous flowers found at any local Korean grocery market, something with color but quite undistinguished. They didn't fool anyone.

"Who are you kidding?" Matson asked, and looked more closely at Roosa. "Lavin's been dead for over a week. What's this, some kind of joke?" He turned the flowers around in his hand and took a sniff. "What the hell are these things for?"

141

"Only way I could figure to get to talk to you."

"About what?"

Roosa took a deep breath and looked directly into the other man's eyes. They looked clear enough, at least for now.

"About a problem you've been having, but really about how Adrian used that knowledge to threaten you. Maybe we should go into your apartment."

"Hold it," the pilot said. "We're not going anywhere. Lavin didn't know, didn't mention, and certainly didn't threaten me with anything. We just talked about the church, my job, and what I do when I finish flying and am back in town."

"You know," Roosa said slowly, "I got the same problem. It's real difficult admitting it, especially to yourself. But this is important. Adrian's dead, and he was killed because of something he knew."

"What the hell is this? What problem are you talking about?"

"You want me to spell it out?" Roosa narrowed his eyes. "Okay. From what I understand, you're a man who likes to drink, and I don't mean root beer. It took me a long time to admit I had a problem. That's a sign of a true alcoholic, so maybe you're still in that stage." Roosa took a breath, then continued. "Anyway, Lavin knew about it, he had it in his notes. The way I figure it, he probably used it to blackmail you. That's an easy one. There can't be too many alcoholic pilots flying these days."

"Shit, old man, what do you know? They're flying, they just don't get caught, that's all."

"Like you?"

Matson's face turned angry. "I don't drink and fly. That would be real stupid, wouldn't it? In fact, I don't drink now, period. I don't want anyone spreading lies about that. I don't know where you're from, or what sort of crap Lavin told you before he got mugged, but it has nothing to do with me. I'm clean." He handed the flowers back to Roosa and stepped back into the doorway of the apartment. "Now beat it."

Roosa held the flowers in one hand, and with the other reached into his jacket pocket and removed a half-full bottle of Thunderbird. He held it up to show him.

"Then you wouldn't care to join me in a toast to the dear departed Mr. Lavin?" The pilot's eyes locked on the wine and followed the bottle as Roosa lifted it for a swig.

"I told you," the pilot hissed, "I don't drink." The door slammed in Roosa's face with such force that the old man dropped the flowers. But he kept his firm grip on the bottle, took another swig, and turned to go.

A man with an alcoholic's eyes and temperament, he thought. A real dry drunk. Takes one to know one. He took another swig, put the bottle back, and went to find his other friends.

# 26

Margaret's apartment sounded like a backroom negotiating session at a political convention. All eight of the friends were there, plus the professor, plus a pizza delivery boy who had just arrived with two large pies, pepperoni and plain. No one made an effort to pick up the greasy check that the young man was holding out so listlessly. Finally Sid rose, took a look at the numbers, and reached for his wallet.

"I'll pay," he offered, "then it's, let's see, two-fifty each."

"That's reasonable," Berdie said. "Including the salad."

"What salad?" Sid asked.

"You didn't get a salad?" She looked scandalized. "I thought we decided to ask for a salad also."

"No salad," Sid repeated. "Don't you remember, there were five no's, three yes's, and one undecided."

Berdie shook her head angrily. "That's right, because you didn't want any. You bullied Rose into a 'no' and Rena abstained because she didn't want to offend anyone.

Humph." She sounded hurt, but nonetheless reached a hand out and got a paper plate and a slice.

"That's democracy," Sid said with grin. "And so is the two-fifty."

"No, not the pepperoni," Berdie said loudly to Pancher, who was handing out the slices. "I won't get any sleep tonight. I wonder who's bright idea that was?" She looked back at Sid.

"We also voted on the pepperoni," Sid said. "You must have been dozing."

"Can we get down to business?" Margaret interrupted. "There are two questions I'd like answered. Did anyone get an impression or even a suspicion that Adrian tried any threats on anybody? And did anyone know Adrian had all that sensitive information about them?" She looked around at the eight other faces and waited patiently while her friends tried to swallow their pizza. Roosa finished first and weighed in with his meeting with Lee Matson, the pilot. When he was finished, Sid summarized his conversation with Nancy Sherwin, closely followed by Rena talking about Peter Sherill, the man with AIDS.

"But no threats?" Margaret asked the three, and they each shook their head adamantly. Then Rose and Durso reported on their interviews with essentially the same negative results. Margaret confirmed what the others had said with her own report.

"Just as I suspected," Margaret summarized. "Adrian was too decent to threaten anyone, even with all the dirt he found out. And from what I'm hearing, they didn't even realize he knew. They all seemed surprised that their secrets had gotten out."

"So, where does that leave us?" Durso asked.

"Right where we began. It could be any one of them. Or for that matter any one of the others," Roosa said.

There was a stunned silence for a moment, pierced only by Berdie asking, "After all that work?"

"I'm not so sure," Professor Guyers finally said. The

eight other people in the room turned towards him. The austerity of his pinstripe suit had been replaced by the casual look of an NYU sweatshirt and blue jeans. In his new outfit he looked more like one of them, even with his combed hair and freshly shaven face. "I'm not so sure," he repeated, and leaned forward. "There's one thing that is standing out so clearly here, I'm surprised no one has picked up on it. Especially you, Margaret."

"Oh," she smiled, "I have, but I haven't figured out the answer. The real question is, if none of the people told him, where was Adrian getting all his information from?"

"Exactly."

"Do you know?" she asked.

Guyers leaned back and scratched his head. "No, not really, but I can make some guesses that might help. We know he was getting some information from the doorman, information about Nancy Sherwin and about Melendez, the illegal alien. So there is precedent there for us to assume he had other sources that he was paying, like the doorman, for sensitive information. I'm not sure that's entirely ethical, Margaret, even if he was only using it in research for a novel. I mean to say, perhaps Adrian was not such an innocent as you have lead us to believe."

Margaret shrugged. "I won't debate that," she said, "you're the professor of ethics. I only maintained he was not the kind to blackmail. Paying for research information . . . that's a different matter."

"So," Professor Guyers continued, "if we assume there was another source for his information, the logical thing to do is find him." He looked around at the others as though they were students around a seminar table. "Isn't that so?"

"How?" Sid asked. "It was just luck that I happened to be friendly with Dominick Spina, even luckier that he was on the door when I came into the building. The odds against us finding another one of his sources are worse than betting on one of the carriage horses in the park to win the Kentucky Derby."

"No, we have to approach it logically and look for associations," Guyers said, "like Sherwin and Morper, who live in the same building. The associations are key."

"But they all don't live in the same building," Berdie interjected."

"There has to be something they have in common," Guyers said. "The fact that they go to the same church is not enough. We have to look elsewhere."

The room was quiet for a while as the nine of them thought. The noise of the traffic outside mixed with the hum of Margaret's refrigerator to produce a white-noise level that drowned out their little movements; their shuffling feet, their face rubs, their hair tugs. No one spoke. No one had an idea.

"Hopeless," Rose said. "Six people with something in common?"

"Five," Margaret said. "Nancy Sherwin came to Adrian via Dominick. Five; one on steroids, one with AIDS, one a drunk, one a cross-dresser, and one an addict."

Guyers looked up slowly. "Medical," he said softly.

"Yeah, but not really," Sid said. "What about the lawyer, the cross-dresser. I'd say it was psychological, or something to do with addiction."

"What about the AIDS patient?" Rena said. "That's no addiction, nor is it psychological."

"I think I got it," Margaret said excitedly. "Of course, how stupid of me! It's right there." She jumped off the sofa and ran to a desk in the corner of the room where Adrian's computer was resting. In a moment she had it working and was running through some text. Her friends were crowding around her shoulders, trying to get a glance at what she was doing.

"What?" Professor Guyers said. "It's in the computer?"

"Yes." She kept scrolling through Adrian's notes, peering at the writing, scrolling some more. Finally she stopped and leaned closer. "Here it is, that first night I did this." She put her finger on the screen and turned around. "Halo. He's right here."

"Halo?" Guyers said. "Could you be more clear? I don't seem to . . ."

"No, you never saw him. He's the druggist," Margaret almost shouted. "He was one of Adrian's subjects, but we haven't gotten to him yet. He's always talking about his clientele and telling Adrian about their patterns of buying. Lots of Alka-Seltzer in the morning and mouthwash in the evening. Look at the last sentence of Adrian's entry: 'The man certainly has a peculiar insider's view of the community.' I think he tapped into that 'peculiar insider's view' for his own book."

"A druggist?" Durso said thoughtfully.

"Sure," Sid snickered. "Who else would know about steroids, methadone, AZT or whatever they use for AIDS."

"And Anabuse," Roosa said. "For alcoholics. You take those pills and the next sip of alcohol you take wrecks you. I tried them once. Tore my head off. I figured the hangovers were much easier."

"What about the cross-dresser?" Berdie asked with a slight blush.

Margaret snapped her fingers. "And I know where Halo works too. When I was talking to Witherspoon, he told me he bought all the panty hose and things at a pharmacy. When I went to his bathroom I couldn't help noticing a big container of sleeping pills on the sink. I remember noticing them. . . . there were so many. And they came from a pharmacy called Kantor's." She colored slightly and looked around. "Well you know me, I'm kind of a nosy-body. Anyway, I'd be very surprised if we don't find our man behind the counter there. Looking over everyone's foibles, selling secrets to Adrian. You're right, William, I'm afraid Adrian did have his lapses." She looked at her watch. "Come on, let's go. If we're lucky maybe he's still there."

"All of us?" Rose asked. "In a tiny drugstore? I know that one, it's no bigger than a candy store."

"You all can wait outside," Margaret said. "Show the

flag. Professor Guyers and I will go in and find out who Halo is, then have a little talk with him."

"He should be fired," Berdie said indignantly. "All those people trusted him."

"Well, maybe he will be," Margaret said, and got up to put on her coat.

# 27

The seven old-timers stood outside Kantor's Drug Store on the corner of West Eighty-seventh Street and Columbus like a rank of soldiers. They pressed their backs against the two parked cars fronting the store and waited silently. Margaret went inside with Professor Guyers. The store was long and narrow, but large enough to have one central display rack and two racks along the side walls. The far end of the store held the druggist's work area and checkout counter. Very basic. The owners of Walgreen Drugs were not spending sleepless nights worrying about competition from Kantor's. Margaret passed by the display of panty hose and waited patiently by the checkout. A young Chinese woman clerk finished giving change for some purchase and then looked up at her.

"Can I speak to the pharmacist?" Margaret asked.

"Just a moment," the young woman said, and retreated behind the partition. In a moment she came back, followed by a middle-aged man in a green smock. His face looked shaved, but by a razor that needed a new head. A patchwork of little hairs remained where he hadn't pressed hard enough. Between them, the skin was sallow and pasty. His eyes looked out from behind wire-rim glasses and were the color of stale coffee. He was short, and the little name tag on his smock told the world that he was Harvey Weiss, pharmacist.

"Yes?" he asked. "Can I help you?"

"Look outside," Margaret said.

"Excuse me?" His eyes narrowed and he frowned, trying to place her request somewhere in the categories of other questions he usually got, like what was the best product for constipation.

"Outside," Margaret nodded behind her. "At all those people." She smiled. "They're my friends."

Finally Mr. Weiss looked up and took in the seven senior citizens lined up against the cars, clearly visible through his front display window.

"They sick?" he asked, still working with his pharamacist's brain.

"No. Just waiting, like Mr. Guyers and me. We're all wondering if you'll do the right thing."

The conversation was moving out of the sphere of the Chinese clerk's job description, so she slid along the counter to help a middle-aged woman at the perfume display. Weiss remained, facing Margaret and Professor Guyers with an expression on his face that was trying to be helpful, but didn't quite comprehend how.

"Do you need a prescription filled?" he asked, reverting to solid ground. That's what he did, filled prescriptions.

"No, I need to get some information from you, information about the kind of things you told Adrian Lavin. I need the names of all those people whose secrets you so carelessly gave away, and just for my own understanding, I'd like to know why a man in your position, someone whom the community trusts, could abuse that trust so flagrantly." She took a breath.

Weiss took a step back and removed his glasses. His face started to show signs of color as his jaw seemed to set into a defiant tightness. "I never told Lavin anything," he said quickly. "Maybe a thing or two about business, but nothing about our clients."

"That is a lie, Mr. Weiss," Professor Guyers said. "And can be proven. To do so, however, would require us to start a class-action civil suit brought on behalf of all your clients, which would be both costly and time consuming."

"A simpler solution," Margaret carried on, "is to notify your boss about your behavior and at the same time run a boycott of your store to bring the point home to him. What do you think it would do to business if your clients had to run a gauntlet of signs pointing out just how far their confidences would be honored? Probably not even to the toothbrush display. How secure would your job be then?"

"It's best you give us what we're asking for," Professor Guyers added. "It will take you five minutes and save you a lot of trouble. Besides, it's used goods; you've already sold it once already."

Weiss looked from one of them to the other, then outside again at Sid and his friends, then put his glasses back on. He motioned them behind the counter and up into his den of pharmacy. When they were behind the partition he turned around and started counting out an order of pills. He was trying to be methodical about his count, but they both could see that his hands were shaking.

"I didn't think it would hurt anybody," he began. "It was all very innocent. Lavin promised he wasn't going to use the names. It would only be background for a novel he was going to write." His head was down over the table and pills, so Margaret couldn't see his expression. His voice, however, if it was any indication, had lost all its power. "I was just telling him about the kind of neighborhood this was, all the crazy people. He was interested in the church and many of them went there."

"People with AIDS, people trying to kick a drug habit or an alcoholic dependency are not crazy," Margaret said with a note of anger in her voice. "I'm surprised you didn't recognize that."

Weiss nodded, head still bowed. "I don't know why I did it."

"For the money, perhaps?" Guyers said.

"Not really." He shrugged and finished counting the pills. He stuck a label on the bottle and put it in a waiting bag. When he turned back his face looked deflated. "Lavin couldn't afford much. It wasn't more than maybe a hundred dollars in total."

"So why then?" Guyers pressed.

"I guess I got tired of counting pills all day in a tiny three-hundred square foot store, listening to people's tales of woe. Constantly, one after another. They thought I was some kind of witch doctor that could cure anything. And let me tell you, I saw it all. Things doctors never see. Little domestic tragedies people want to keep secret. Came a time when I wanted to unburden myself and Adrian was there to listen. To share some of the folly."

"And you told him about everyone?" Margaret asked.

"No, just about the ones that were different, the ones that made good reading. I didn't tell him about the menopausal women with their estrogen, or the insomniacs with their Xanax, or the diabetics, or the hundreds of others. In fact, I only told him about a few."

"Yes," Margaret recited, "Witherspoon, Sherill, Matson, Hanson, and Dena Duval."

"Yes," Weiss said, "and Candovala."

Margaret looked quickly over at Guyers and frowned. "Candovala?"

"Yeah, Juan Candovala. I told Lavin about him last week. Comes in for insulin couple of times a month."

"I thought you passed over the diabetics as being too boring," Guyers said sarcastically.

"Not for that," Weiss said. "He also came in for bandages and antiseptic cream, and sometimes vitamin E cream.

Enough to make me take notice." Weiss lowered his glasses and looked at the two older people in his little cubicle.

"So?" Margaret asked.

"So, it's a little peculiar," Weiss said. "I didn't think too much about it until one day he brought his kid in with him. Little boy about four years old. He needed some eardrops. The child cried a lot and Candovala figured it was an earache. He asked me to look. You know, I'm the local unpaid doctor around here, it's either me or all day in the emergency room. So I came around and took a look. He did have a slight inflammation, enough to cause the crying, but that's not all I saw. He was wearing a loose shirt, and for some reason I glanced down at his neck and upper shoulders, and I saw," he hesitated for a moment, "all these tiny red marks. Each one looked like a double arch, one inside the other and a little shorter, like two C's. I'd never seen anything like that before. Spots are usually circular." He let that sink in. "And then I remembered all that antiseptic, and burn cream he'd been buying. . . . and where I'd seen those shapes before. They were made from one half of a paper clip.

"Oh God!" Margaret said. "He burned the boy?"

Weiss didn't say anything.

"So what did you do?" Professor Guyers asked.

"I asked Candovala about them, but he just mumbled something about an allergy and paid for the eardrops and left. He hasn't been back since."

"You didn't tell the police?" Guyers was frowning.

"What if I was wrong? I mean, I only saw five or six of them. Maybe they were some peculiar birthmark. I could get in big trouble for accusing someone falsely."

"You said nothing?" Margaret asked. "Nothing at all?"

"I told Lavin," the pharmacist said embarrassedly. "I told Lavin because, well, maybe I thought he might do something."

"No." Margaret shook her head. The color had risen in her cheeks and she was pointing a finger at the younger man. "You told Lavin because you just wanted to pass off your guilt to someone else. You wanted to feel better about not doing anything in the face of this horrendous abuse. Adrian had already told you he wasn't going to do anything with your information except record it, so it was just a matter of passing the buck, or burned child to be more exact. You are, Mr. Weiss, a despicable person and should be punished. Unfortunately, there are no laws against what you didn't do for that poor child, but your conscience, if you still have one, should be taken out and whipped." Margaret caught her breath. "Now," she continued. "There is one thing you must do, and that is give us Candovala's address. At least you can do that."

"You mean give the address of one of my customers to total strangers?" He shook his head.

Guyers slammed his hand down on the work counter and a dozen jars of pills danced their contents for a second. "You have the gall to hide behind ethics. That is quite outrageous. Besides, you must have given it to Adrian."

Weiss was silent.

"Good lord," Margaret said. "He must have gone to see him."

Weiss shrugged. "He never said he did, but then again, come to think of it, I never saw Lavin after I gave him the address."

"Something happened there," Margaret added, "I know it. Cross-dressers, alcoholics," she shook her head, "are one thing. Child abusers are quite another. Adrian might not have been able to resist confronting him." She looked directly at the pharmacist now and her voice dropped a note. She talked very slowly. "The address."

At that moment, the young Chinese clerk stuck her head around the partition and asked if everything was okay. Guyers's explosion had brought her over. Weiss looked at her forlornly, and nodded. As she retreated back to the cash register, Weiss took one more look at Margaret, then went to his files. In a moment he had the address.

Guyers copied it down. "One last thing, Mr. Weiss," he

said. "I would rethink my role in the community if I were you. It does little good to dispense eardrops to a child of brutal chronic abuse. If you're tired of counting pills, think of how tired little Candovala is of getting burned." He turned to Margaret and the two of them moved away from the pharmacy area and headed out to their friends. Weiss watched them for a long moment, unable to go back to his counting pills.

On the street, Margaret turned to Guyers before her friends could come up.

"I want to get a look at that child before I tell the police about Candovala. All I have is the pharmacist's word."

"And how do you plan to do that?" Guyers asked.

She smiled innocently. "I know just the person to help," she said. "Peter Frangapani. And tomorrow's just the right day."

# 28

When Juan Candovala opened his door the next afternoon, he was greeted by a little boy in a Cub Scout uniform and an older woman holding a shopping bag. Little seven-year-old Peter Frangapani had no idea why he had been brought up the four flights in this strange building after his Cub Scout meeting, but Margaret had asked him merely to stand by the front door for a few minutes and smile. Hey, that was easy.

Candovala was a short man with a moustache and a face pockmarked by some childhood disease. His hair was long and drawn into a ponytail. Margaret guessed that he was somewhere around thirty-five, although she wouldn't be surprised at forty. He wore blue jeans and a work shirt that had the inscription "Munoz's Muffler Shop" on it. His dark eyes looked at her suspiciously. All in all, he gave the impression of being unfriendly, the kind of person to be trusted with machines, perhaps, not children. But there was a child there, back in the corner of the living room. A little boy of about four years old watching television.

"Yeah," Candovala said, looking down at little Peter.

"You are Mr. Candovala?" Margaret began. "I was told you lived in this apartment with your son. Oh, there he is," she said. "May I come in? I'd like to tell you something about the Cub Scouts."

"Cub who?"

"Scouts. Certainly you've heard of them." Margaret took a tentative step forward into the apartment. The little boy watching television looked up for a moment, then went back to his cartoons. "Cub Scouts are a wonderful way for your son to learn about nature and the world around him. It gives him a chance to go camping a few times a year, and it's especially good to bring fathers and sons closer together." She smiled. "Or mothers and sons. Are you married, Mr. Candovala?"

"Carlos's mother is dead," he said simply. "But your kid looks a lot older. And, you don't look like no mother of his."

"Quite right," Margaret said. "I'm his mother's friend. Like you, I suppose, she's alone with the child. But that shouldn't stop you. It's only one afternoon a week. We meet every Tuesday over at the church on West Eighty-ninth Street." She took another step inside and looked around quickly. The apartment appeared to be a single room with a kitchen. Dirty dishes were stacked up from several meals, and the garbage can was overflowing. The room itself held a large bed and a sofa, a table, some chairs, and the television set. On the floor were a few meager children's toys on a patterned rug. The place was messy, but the furniture looked solid and store-bought, not scrounged from the garbage. Her gaze came down to little Carlos.

"How old is your son?" she asked.

"He will be five next month. But I don't think he has time for no Cub Scouts. Me neither. Besides, ain't he too young?"

"Let's see." Margaret reached into her shopping bag and withdrew a small blue shirt with insignias on it, one of Peter's earlier Cub Scout uniforms. In a flash, she had taken the five steps across the room and bent down to hold the shirt up to the little boy. She measured it against his back, then against his front while he squirmed away to keep watching the television.

"Hey, what you doing?" Candovala said, and took a few steps nearer.

Margaret's body was between the boy and his father, and in the two seconds it took for him to come over, she pulled the front of his T-shirt down to get a look at his chest. When Candovala got next to her, she was stretching the Cub Scout shirt tight across Carlos's front.

"Yes, he is a little young. This is the smallest shirt, and you can see it is still too large. I think maybe he'll have to wait a year. Maybe when he is six years old." She stood up and turned to the man with the ponytail. "Our troop is a little undersubscribed, and we are doing everything we can to recruit new members. So when I heard that you had a little boy, I thought I would see if I could convince you to send him. But you are right, he is too young."

"I told you, he don't have the time anyway. Neither do I. Now, maybe you want to leave and take your kid with you."

"Certainly," Margaret said, and walked back to the front door. "Thanks anyway for your time." Her eyes narrowed as she grabbed little Peter's hand, and they turned through the door. They continued to hear the sound of the Candovala television all the way to the elevator.

"What was that about?" Peter asked. "We got more kids in our troop than we have room for."

"For the future," Margaret said, and breathed easier when the elevator doors had closed. But she knew she wasn't finished with Juan Candovala. The red welts she had seen on Carlos's chest, clearly like the pharmacist had described, wouldn't let her walk away. She presumed Adrian had had the same response. But now Adrian's murder receded in her mind as the ongoing fate of the little boy Carlos became painfully clear.

"No time for Cub Scouts," she repeated to herself softly. "We'll see about that." As she exited the building and walked down the block, still holding Peter's hand, she was unaware of Candovala looking at her from the fourth-floor window, looking at her and frowning.

# 29

Detective Laura Green looked across her desk the next morning at the white-haired older lady. Margaret had set up the appointment an hour earlier by telephone, and it had taken her that long to trudge downtown to Homicide headquarters. The first thing she did after sitting down was light a cigarette. There was already so much smoke in the air that she didn't worry about adding her own. Scratch was at the next desk and glanced over casually, but Sniff motioned him off with her eyes. No need, she thought, to bring in the shock troops on this old bird. Edwards was still smarting from Renzuli's decision to let Hector Melendez go. This had come when Melendez managed to produce a belated alibi from someone working a bar in Spanish Harlem. Normally that kind of alibi is as worthless as a disclaimer at an amusement park, except that the particular bartender in question had a good sheet with the precinct boys up in his neighborhood. Renzuli, as a rule, hated these eleventh hour alibis, but this one was good enough to change his thinking on things. So the book was still open on Lavin's murder, and on several others that had come in since. Green and Edwards had just caught one that morning that was going to require a lot of legwork. The policewoman looked down at her watch and asked, as politely as she could, what Margaret had in mind.

"I know you're working on the Lavin murder; Lieutenant Morley told me, so I thought you might be interested to learn that I just found out who killed Adrian." She took a deep puff of her cigarette and waited for the tall woman to take down all the information. Instead, Laura Green smiled, still the model of politeness, and asked Margaret how it was she came by this information.

"Did he confess?" she asked.

"Not exactly." Margaret frowned. "In fact we never talked about it. I just know, that's all, from all the other things. . . . from Carlos's condition."

Laura Green leaned back and looked at the older woman carefully. "Perhaps you better start at the beginning," she said. "Who's Carlos?"

Margaret nodded. "Yes, I see that. Just the name Juan Candovala is not enough." She crushed out the cigarette and cleared her throat. Then she told Officer Green all she could about her investigation and about her discussion with the pharmacist. She concluded by relating her brief visit with Candovala and Carlos. When she was finished, she sat back and waited.

"It's not enough," Sniff said. "I wish it were, but it's not. You need a lot more than speculation, logic, inference, or hearsay. You need hard facts." She took a deep breath. "And as far as I can tell, the only fact that you have is a bunch of little burns on a boy's chest. You don't know Adrian ever went to visit, you don't know if he did whether he threatened Candovala or not, and you certainly have no proof that Candovala was even at the scene of the crime, much less that he struck the fatal blow. Unless our witness," she flipped some of her notes, "the woman who was casually glancing out of her sixth-floor window, can make an identification, you have nothing. In fact, even less than we had on the man we caught with Lavin's wallet." She shook her head. "I'm afraid, Mrs. Binton, this is, if anything, only a start."

"You've got to be kidding." Margaret was unbelieving. "Only a start?"

"On the murder, that is. But I think you've certainly given us enough to investigate him for child abuse. Especially when we take a look at the kid to confirm the burn marks." She smiled somewhat ruefully. "Only problem is, I'm in Homicide, not Child Welfare. I've got to pass this on."

"No," Margaret grimaced. "I know how these things work. They get lost like that. Maybe a month from now a rookie beat policeman will accompany some very overworked social worker to Candovala's apartment, at which time Carlos will either be dead or disfigured. And by a murderer who the police know about. You can't let that happen. You can't." She must have raised her voice because Edwards got up from his desk and sauntered over.

"A problem here?" he asked.

Green was holding Margaret's eyes, and for a moment she didn't answer. "No, Sonny, I got it under control." She looked up at her partner. "We got to be over on the Upper West Side later today, don't we?" Scratch nodded. "So okay, how about we make a detour. Mrs. Binton here might have shed some light on the Lavin thing." She looked back at Margaret. "And besides, I hate men that beat up on little kids. The sooner we get to him the better."

Margaret smiled, but her face was still flushed.

"Thank you," she said.

"But, I'm telling you, a murder conviction is harder to get to stick than glue to an ice cube. That's why there's so much plea bargaining around. Even if things are what you say, maybe we'll have to settle for a lesser charge. An A-one felony can be fifteen to twenty-five years minimum. Can't do much better on a murder two." She looked over to her partner. "Guy is burning paper clips into his four-year-old son.

If we find things are like she says, we can grab the kid, bring him to Child Welfare?"

"Why, we're not busy enough?" Edwards said sarcastically. "We're gonna play nursemaid all afternoon? Those things take hours."

"I can spare a couple of hours for an abused kid." Green looked back at Margaret. "Give me your phone number, then go home. We'll call later this afternoon after seeing Candovala and putting his name through the Albany master list of known child abusers. Don't worry, he won't know you had anything to do with this. I'll work out an angle."

"Thanks," Margaret said, scribbling the number down on a pad in front of her, and got up to go. "I really am convinced he killed Adrian Lavin, you know. I sensed it. But I couldn't bring myself to ask if he knew him. I was," she hesitated, "just a little scared."

"You've already done enough," Green said. "Now let the professionals take over."

# 30

Margaret was furious when she got off the phone with Detective Green four hours later. The phrase "there's nothing more we can do" still buzzed in her ear like an angry bee trapped inside a water glass. That had come after Green reported that Candovala wasn't on the Albany master list of child abusers, although he had a sheet for two previous drug arrests. But he had done his time in Greenhaven, and had apparently been clean for years. The real disappointment came when the woman detective reported that Carlos was not at the apartment, taking any evidence of abuse with him. "Child Welfare is looking into it," Green had concluded. "There's nothing more we can do now. The apartment was clean and neat, and Candovala told us Carlos is staying with a friend. She picked him up this morning. Without the kid, we're stymied."

"Do you have an address or phone number where he went?" Margaret asked.

"A phone number, but it's been busy for the last half hour. You want, you can try it." She read the number to

Margaret. "I also gave that to Child Welfare. Then I asked Candovala if he ever heard of Lavin and I got the blankest of responses. . . . too blank, frankly, so Edwards and I grilled him for another fifteen minutes, but came away empty. Sorry, Mrs. Binton. That was the best I could give it. We're so overloaded that Edwards was tugging on me the whole time."

But that was not the best Margaret could do. Or so she told Guyers when she called him a minute later.

"Carlos was sent away. I assume he is being hidden. I just want to know, legally, if I can force the Child Welfare people to take action if I can find him."

"If there's evidence of abuse," the professor said. "If there's not, or if it's sketchy, you could be opening a can of worms. Last year two sets of parents filed federal suits for a total of twenty-two million dollars against the Human Resource Administration, its head, the case workers for the agency that did the foster placement, and even the foster parents for illegal seizure of their children. I suppose that's made everyone involved in the process from the bottom to the top very jittery. But that's what the system is set up for, might as well use it."

"So I just have to find the child," she said softly, almost to herself.

There was silence on the line for a moment. Finally he came back. "How about if I come over in an hour? This is not the kind of thing you should be doing on your own."

"Thank you, William," Margaret said with feeling. "I suppose you're right. I have a few calls to make, but after that I'll be waiting." She was about to hang up when she remembered something.

"Sweatshirt," she said.

"Of course. I wouldn't dream of anything else."

She hung the phone up and looked at the number she had been given by Green, the place where Carlos was supposed to be staying. She spent over fifteen minutes dialing and redialing until she was convinced that there was some

166

mistake. Finally, when she was about to give up, she heard a click on the other end and a recording started playing.

"Hello, you have reached Sports Phone, your daily score update computerized service. For last minute scores of the New York Yankees, press one, for the New York Mets, press two, for . . ." Margaret frowned and hung up the phone quickly. What had Green said, "Let the professionals handle it"? What a joke. She leaned back and closed her eyes for a long moment, trying to remember something.

"He had something on. . . ." She concentrated hard, as hard as she ever did reaching for one of those obscure *New York Times* crosswords. She had seen it, but what did it say, in little script, over the pocket? Finally she opened her eyes with a smile.

"Munoz's Muffler Shop. That's what his shirt said." Once again she reached for the phone.

# 31

Munoz's Muffler Shop was located on West 126th Street, near the West Side Highway overpass. By the time Margaret and Guyers arrived it was past 4:00 and there was only one person working in the shop. Mufflers of all size and shape were stacked in metal shelves to one side, and overhead there was an equal number of shapes for the tail pipes. Munoz's was doing its best to compete with the larger chains like Midas and Meineke, and by the looks of things it was having modest success. There were four cars waiting repair and a time clock by the side door indicated there were more than eight employees employed to do the work. Margaret and the professor walked tentatively over to the single employee who was studying a mechanical part resting on a side desk. He looked up and frowned at the sight of the two older people.

"Yeah?" he said questioningly.

"Do you have a gentleman working for you by the name of Juan Candovala?" Margaret asked.

He took his eyes off them and studied the part on the bench more closely. "Maybe," he said. "Why?"

"Oh, it's nothing he's done," Margaret said quickly. "It's just that his aunt and my friend here and I were at the same senior citizens center yesterday. We were sitting around playing canasta and chatting, talking about grandchildren and relatives, when the woman mentioned that her nephew, Juan, worked here." She stopped for a breath. "Isn't that right, William?"

"Precisely," Guyers said seriously. "Canasta."

"No, I mean Munoz's Muffler Shop over on One hundred and twenty-sixth," Margaret corrected him. "So, don't you see, when she got up from the table and left her eyeglasses behind, we really had no other way to find her. I've never seen her before at our center. I suppose we could have left them at the lost and found, but quite frankly," she leaned closer, "I don't trust Mr. Blessington, who's in charge of that. I think he steals things right from the lost and found himself." She straightened up. "I don't live too far away, so we thought we'd come to find out Juan's address and maybe, if we're lucky, the address of his aunt. Or maybe someone who knows the aunt. You don't mind, do you? These glasses were something special, wait'll you see." She rummaged in her large handbag until she came out with a pair of her late husband's glasses, the ones with lenses heavy enough to start a brushfire. "See, she'd be lost without them," Margaret concluded.

"Candovala, eh?" The man turned back, took a glance at the glasses, and then peered up at the two people in front of him. If they had been policemen he might have tried to put the bite on them, but as it was, it didn't look like the two together had enough to tip a taxi driver. In fact, the man looked kind of thrown together in a sweatshirt and baggy trousers. He gave up on that tack and decided to play it straight.

"Yeah, Candovala works here four, five days a week. I suppose I could get you an address." He raised himself tiredly off of his chair and went over to a small office by a corner of the shop. Margaret and Guyers followed. In a file cabinet he found a sheaf of papers and went through it slowly. Finally he pulled one out and glanced over it.

"Here it is," he said, "One-oh-three West Ninety-ninth Street. Then there's a section down at the bottom where we ask for a contact in case of emergency. No aunt, but he's listed some man by the name of Nestor Benitez."

"An address or phone number?" Margaret asked. "Maybe it's the aunt's husband."

"One thirty-nine West One hundred thirty-seventh Street." He closed the file and put it back. "I hope that's what you need, because I gotta go back and finish this job. I promised the car by five."

"Thank you," they both said in unison, then turned to go.

"You ever need a muffler repaired, you know where to come," the man said, walking back to the bench.

"I ever need a muffler repaired you'll have to do it with knitting needles," she answered.

# 32

Nestor Benitez lived in a small walk-up apartment not too far from the muffler shop. The neighborhood was mixed, and included children playing on the street, grown men loitering, and housewives doing late afternoon shopping. Margaret was not too happy with the three-flight walk-up, nor the condition of the stairwell with its dark recesses, but she felt better when the door finally opened and a man looked out at them with a friendly face. He was short, had a little patch of bald showing through a fringe of gray hair, and was holding a spatula in his hand. An apron ringed his midriff and a smell of cooking onions and peppers wafted past him. When he opened his mouth to talk, which he did when he saw the two strangers at his door, a spot of gold gleamed out from a front tooth. Margaret put him at about fifty.

"You with the Welfare Department?" he asked right off.

"No, we're not with any agency. We're just looking for Carlos," Margaret said.

"Carlos?" the man looked genuinely puzzled.

"Carlos Candovala," Professor Guyers replied. "Little boy, about four years old."

"Oh, Juan's son. I thought you was looking for someone older. What's he done now?"

"Carlos hasn't done anything," Margaret said.

"No, I mean Juan. That boy is always getting into one thing or another." He shook his head. "He was a problem from the day he was born."

"You are related?" Margaret asked.

"Cousins," Mr. Benitez supplied. "Fifteen years younger than me, but I guess I'm the closest relative he has. His mother died back in 'sixty-nine. Liver gave out from all the cheap whiskey she was drinking. But then, if I had a son like that, I'd be drinking too." He looked down at his spatula and seemed to remember something. "Hold on," he added, and turned back into the apartment. In a minute he was back, this time without the spatula. "Burned onions no good for anyone. How come you looking for Carlos?"

Margaret cleared her throat. "Actually, Juan works on my car a lot, and last week he asked me if I could look after his son for a couple of days when he was going out of town. I told him the best I could do was a day trip to the zoo or something. He said that would be okay, and that when I was ready maybe I could find Carlos here." She stopped for a breath. "Tomorrow is a good day for us, so I thought I'd come by to make arrangements." She shrugged. "I guess he found somewhere else to put him?"

"That's real surprising," the man with the gold tooth said. "He's never asked me to take him. I wouldn't know the first thing about a kid that age. No," he shook his head. "Couple of times I heard he found someone over at Spiders to take the kid for a night or two. You know, some of those women got their own children and know what to do. Not me. I can cook up a plate of vegetables, but that's about it."

"Spiders?" Margaret asked with a frown.

The man looked at her closely. "I guess he didn't want to tell you about that place. It's a bar over on One hundred

172

and sixth Street. Pool table in back. He hangs out there a lot. It's not the kind of place that's gonna win any awards for charm, if you know what I mean." He winked. "It's strictly business; booze, blues, and broads. I think there was a woman called Marita. . . . something like that. Maybe the kid's with her?"

"A bar?" Margaret repeated doubtfully. There was silence for a moment. "What happened to Carlos's mother?" she finally asked.

The man chuckled. "She stayed around for a couple of years. Long enough to show Carlos off to every crack dealer on Amsterdam Avenue. Then one day she got hold of some bad stuff and Juan wound up a single parent. I guess people around my cousin wind up in trouble one way or another. That's why I keep my distance. You know he once knifed a guy?" He nodded. "He did, but he got off. Self-defense or some other nonsense like that."

Margaret exchanged glances with Guyers. "Here in the city?" she asked.

"Puerto Rico. It's not on his record or nothing, it's just something to watch out for. I'm telling you because you look like a nice couple of people. It's nice of you to think of the kid, but Juan . . ." he shook his head.

"I understand," Margaret said. "Thank you."

"What zoo?"

"Excuse me?" Margaret said.

"What zoo was you going to take the kid to?"

"Central Park," Margaret said. "But first we gotta find him."

The man shrugged. "Try Spiders," he said. "And if you find him, let me know. After all, the kid's my second cousin, right? I might like to join you."

"First cousin, once removed," Margaret said, correcting him. "But don't worry, no one ever gets that right."

# 33

By the time Margaret and Professor Guyers found the bar called Spiders, it was past 6:00. They had spent half an hour searching for the address unsuccessfully in the phone book, and then decided to just walk the streets looking for it. One hundred and sixth was a long stretch of pavement, but they concentrated on the western part, closest to Broadway. They passed a lot of take-out chicken shops, clothing stores specializing in discount acetates, smoke shops, and even a few bars, but nothing called Spiders. After a half-hour of fruitless search, Margaret decided to break down and ask someone.

The first three people had no idea, but she got lucky with the fourth. A middle-aged man in a pair of blue jeans and work shirt pointed east, and said it was next to a garage.

"There's a plastic sign in the window, and next to it a picture of a black widow," he said. "You can't miss it." But they almost did, since the sign had been slanted outward and the picture of the black widow could have easily been mistaken for a spray-paint exercise. Guyers peered in the window, but there was a set of dusty curtains keeping the inside from view. He went to the door, opened it, and waited for Margaret to follow. Inside they found themselves in a large room with a bar along one wall. There were a few empty tables, a jukebox in the corner, a tired, chipped, mirrored ball overhead, and some badly framed posters which had, as far as Margaret could tell, no unifying theme. In one a cowboy was swinging a rope, in another a koala bear was posed in a tree, and a third showed a quarterback cocking his arm for a pass. Not a spider, or an insect motif in sight, unless you counted the very real cockroach Margaret spotted underneath one of the tables. A door led off to the right, where the pool table must have been. The sound of colliding balls made it out to the front room, where there were only a few people to take notice. Besides themselves, three men and one woman were sitting at the bar amidst a swirl of cigarette smoke, while the bartender lounged a few feet away. Margaret lit one of her own Camels nervously, and when she looked back up, she noticed five sets of eyes watching her. She ambled over and took a stool, while Guyers slid onto the one next to her. The black bartender looked at them for a long moment, then decided to come over.

"Jack Daniel's on the rocks," Margaret said without hesitating. "With a twist."

"Scotch," Guyers said.

He nodded casually and went over to the bottles. A few moments later he was back with two glasses. He was a tall man who could have played linebacker for the Giants if they'd been recruiting from the over-fifty set. The glasses looked like children's toys in his meaty hands.

"You from around here?" he asked lazily.

"Checking out the local color," Guyers said nervously. He was still watching the other people in the room stealing glances at them.

"Well, then, you came to the wrong place," the other man said. "Only color in this joint is in the water."

"We're looking for a little boy called Carlos," Margaret

175

said quickly. "Juan Candovala's son." She took a full drink from the bourbon and continued. "Someone told us he might be staying with one of the women who frequent this establishment."

The big bartender tilted his head back and laughed. "The last person who called this place an establishment was the sanitation inspector, and he was looking for his fifty-dollar handshake," he said. "This ain't no 'establishment.' " He mopped the bar in front of him casually. "So you're looking for Candovala's son." He stood up straight and studied them in silence. After a full minute he continued. "What, are you some kind of social workers or something?"

Professor Guyers shook his head. "Just friends. We want to take him to the zoo."

"Sure," the bartender said, "and I'm Jackie Robinson. The zoo? Who you kidding?" He laughed again but this time not so loudly. "You be straight with me, you find you get further."

Margaret took a deep breath. "Yes, you're right. The truth is we want to make sure he's all right. His father sent him away when the Child Welfare people came, and that made us worry. Candovala has a bad temper and I'm afraid that sometimes he takes it out on Carlos." Margaret looked steadily in the bartender's eyes. She finished her drink and put the glass back on the bar with a noise. She nodded in the direction of Professor Guyers. "This gentleman is a lawyer and capable of seeing that no further harm comes to the boy, legally. If he's staying with someone you know about, you'd be doing Carlos a favor by telling us."

The bartender was silent for a moment, studying her.

"What's a couple of old-timers gonna do?" he finally said.

"Leave that to us," Guyers said. "Seems to me it's about time someone stood up for what's right." Guyers sounded angry enough to draw an admiring stare from Margaret.

The bartender looked more serious. He leaned forward

again, glanced toward the other people at the bar, then lowered his voice.

"Yeah, I suppose maybe you're right. Go find Marissa, she's upstairs. Short, dark complexion, little scar on her chin. I think she's got him for a few days. That's all I know. What Candovala does with his son," he shrugged, "is none of my business."

"Marissa," Margaret repeated.

"Second floor in the back." He nodded. "She lives with two other women and their kids, but you can't miss her. She's the one with the big heart."

# 34

The apartment was right over the bar. It was one of those railroad flats with the front room leading right into another and then another in a straight line until it ended at the fire exit out the back window. This apartment had apparently been broken up into three separate living spaces with one common bathroom. Marissa's was in the back, so Margaret and Guyers had to walk through two bed-sitting rooms before they got to the tiny space that was hers. It was furnished with a bed, a couch, a Formica table, a wire bookcase with books and a television, and an abundance of religious pictures. Carlos was on the couch watching television, and the woman sitting next to him looked exactly as the bartender had described her.

''These two people looking to see you,'' said the woman who had showed them back.

Marissa got up and came over looking curious. The scar on her chin was small, only about an inch long, and not too deep, but perhaps still a vivid reminder of some old argument. It looked like it had been made with a sharp knife.

"Hello," Margaret said. "I've met Carlos before, but we've never had the pleasure." The woman looked behind her for a moment at the little boy, then held her hand out.

"Marissa Fernandez," she said.

The two women shook hands. "My name's Margaret Binton. This is my friend William Guyers. We've come, really, to find Carlos. I was worried about him. . . . with Candovala."

Marissa Fernandez's eyes narrowed and looked from one of them to the other.

"About what?"

Margaret took a deep breath. "I saw some red marks on Carlos two days ago. They looked very much like . . . burn marks."

Marissa turned away and went to the back window. She looked out through the bars and the fire escape at a wiry acanthus tree snaking its branches everywhere. Her head was shaking slowly from side to side as her hand went up to her forehead.

"I have talked to Juan about this," she said finally. "Several times. I have even threatened to report him. And still it goes on."

"Why don't you?" Guyers asked curiously.

Marissa turned and faced them. "I don't think you'd understand. Juan and me . . . well," she shrugged, "he takes care of me. I don't want to lose that."

"I can see that," Margaret said. "Did he give you the cut?" Margaret tapped her own chin.

The other woman grimaced. "That was my fault. I was holding back some money that was his." She sniffed and wiped her eye with the back of her hand. "Most of the times he can be very gentle."

"Did you ever ask Carlos that?" Guyers said.

Marissa flashed her eyes at him, but the professor was not about to look away.

"I do what I can," she said. "If I reported him they'd take Carlos away and that would kill Juan. He is a good man.

179

He just gets carried away sometimes. All alone with the boy ever since that crackhead mother died. And when it gets too much for him, I try to help. I've never said no."

"But it continues," Margaret said. "The abuse. Don't you think it would be better to play judge rather than nurse? Stop what's happening rather than pick up the pieces after the damage is done?" There was a note of anger in her voice. "The little boy is being tortured and you look on."

"I don't look on, I take him. Besides, I try to change Juan. It doesn't happen lately that often, I swear." She looked back out the window. "I protect Carlos all I can."

"When Candovala calls. What happens when he doesn't?"

The other woman was silent. "I try to check."

"Well, I think you could be doing a better job," Margaret said. "And if you can't, it's time for others to step in. Candovala has no power over me or my friend. And we're here to help you too, help you do what you should have done a long time ago."

"You're very important in all this." Guyers added. "You'll have to corroborate that this is not just a single occurrence, that it's a pattern."

Marissa Fernandez looked back at the little boy who was so intent on the television. None of the marks could be seen, and from all outward appearances, he looked quite normal.

"What will happen to me?" she asked softly.

"You're not the boy's parent," Guyers said. "I don't think you'll have a problem. Legally. If this is done quickly and quietly. Not from the outside, anyway."

"There's always Juan, you mean?"

"There's that. But you can seek help if you are afraid of him."

She laughed. At least it started out as a laugh and ended up as sort of a choked cry. *"Ay! Dios mio!* My cousin had a problem with a man and she was given protection too. She is now in a very fine plot in the cemetery. Don't talk to me about protection."

"If the case is strong enough, and I think it is," Professor Guyers said, "Candovala will go to prison. You will not have to worry."

"Until he gets out and comes looking for me."

"You are the person who took care of his child," Margaret said. "You are the person that saved him from himself. Certainly, he'll come to see that. And then there's always Carlos. It's about time someone worried about his problems."

Marissa went over to the couch and the little boy. She sat down slowly, put her arms around him and hugged him. He looked up, then over curiously at the two strangers, then he went back to watching the television.

"It was only a little bit at first," Marissa said slowly. "A few small bruises, nothing that a thousand other parents don't do. The paper clips . . ." she shook her head. "That only started this year. The red marks you saw, they mostly go away in a week or two. It looks worse than it is."

"Would you like them put on your body?" Margaret asked.

There was a long silence, then Marissa said, "It's gotta stop. I know that. I don't know if I'm strong enough to do it myself. Juan is just . . ." she left the thought unspoken.

"Marissa, this is not going to go unreported," Margaret said tightly. "Whatever you decide to do, I'm still picking up the phone and calling the police now that I've found Carlos. What you do however, will put you on one side of the line or the other. That's the way I see it, and that's the way the police will too." There was silence in the room for a long moment.

"What do you want me to do?" Marissa finally said.

"I'll call from here," Margaret said. "The Child Welfare people will be here hopefully within the hour. We'll wait with you. Just tell your story the way you told it to us. After that," she looked over at her friend, "I don't know what happens."

Marissa looked nervously from one to the other, closed her eyes for a moment, then seemed to shrug some weight

181

off. When she opened her eyes again she had a harder look to her face.

"Men," she smiled sadly, "the moment I keep a little extra something to pay for all the money I spent on Carlos, he gives me this." She touched her scar.

"Where'd the money come from?" Margaret asked simply. "The money he gave you."

Marissa fussed with a wisp of her hair. Finally she confessed. "Numbers and stuff like that. Juan lived too nicely to be satisfied with what he made only at that garage. He had a few people out collecting for him. I wasn't the only one. But it wasn't nothing big. He kept a few hundred a week."

"That was all? Did he ever sell drugs?" Guyers asked.

Marissa shook her head. "No way man, he was afraid of that. He's been busted selling drugs twice, and he knew the next time would land him in jail for a long time. No, only numbers; sometimes he'd take on a little fencing, that was it."

Margaret remembered Detective Green telling her of Candovala's previous drug record. "And child abuse," Margaret added pointedly.

"Yes," Marissa said sadly. She looked back up and smiled bravely. "Make the call," she said. "Before I change my mind. Then I will go and make some coffee while we wait."

"Just what I was going to suggest," Margaret said, and went to look for the phone.

# 35

The New York City Human Resources Administration and its Child Welfare division is massive, arbitrary, underfunded, and populated by harassed, lifeless caseworkers. But most of all, it is notoriously sluggish. It was nothing short of amazing, then, that precisely twenty-five minutes after Margaret placed the call the doorbell rang, and one of the CWA workers presented himself. And not just any worker: a large black man with the light of intelligence shining behind his brown eyes, and enough bulk to take command of most any situation. His name was Westgate, and in five minutes he had everything under control. The luck of the draw. Westgate knew the law, knew his options, knew what was best for Carlos, and knew how to negotiate through the city's rickety structure of children's caregiving institutions to the nearest and best shelter. The immediate result was that Marissa relinquished Carlos into temporary foster care, the only way Juan could be kept from getting his hands back on his son for the time being. Since Marissa was neither a relative nor had been approved by the city as a foster care parent, she would not qualify. She argued as much as she could, but Westgate refused after seeing the red welts, and threatened to call a policeman if she insisted. He took a detailed account from Marissa and from Margaret and Professor Guyers before collecting the little boy and getting him ready to go. As difficult as the parting was for Marissa, Westgate was very creative in making the separation less painful for Carlos. He told him about all the new friends he was going to make, and all the new toys. Carlos, a child battered by a father who also dropped him off at strange places at irregular intervals, left without complaint. Westgate promised Marissa he would notify her when Carlos's case came up, especially if there was a hearing on a preliminary motion to terminate parental rights. He told her she would have to testify in family court as to what she had observed, along with Mrs. Binton, and that she should try to be as specific as possible. Then he lifted Carlos up in his arms and vanished through the door. Margaret and Professor Guyers stayed on, trying to make Marissa feel better, but nothing they did seemed to help or stay the growing sense of fear that was creeping into her expression. Now that Carlos was gone, it was obvious that she was concentrating on Juan. After another forty-five minutes they felt as though they were talking to a stone wall, so they said good-bye.

By the time they got back to Margaret's apartment it was late. Neither of them had eaten, so Margaret threw some Stouffer's dinners into the oven and quickly set the table.

"I hope you don't mind," she said. "It's too late for me to start in on something creative."

"Hell, I'll go you one further," Guyers confessed. "I just buy the cans. No pretense there. Stouffer's is a step up." He grinned and helped Margaret with the plates. In a few minutes they were eating a tuna casserole with broccoli béarnaise and candied carrots.

"Delicious," Professor Guyers said. "And I thank you for the invitation." He took another bite of the whitish mass of glutinous protein and savored the flavor for a moment.

"And I also thank you for allowing me to accompany you today. I find what we did far more significant than teaching continuing education students the ins and outs of ethics."

"That's important too," Margaret said between bites. "And I'm not so sure how effective what we did today really is. There's a possibility that the system will find a way to send Carlos back to Candovala. Maybe if he promises to see a psychologist and go to counseling, or have a social worker look in once a month." She made a face. "As far as I'm concerned, he should never be allowed to see that boy again. Besides, he's a murderer."

"But you can't prove it."

"No, I can't," she said with frustration in her voice, "and it's getting me really angry."

"Which is one reason you did what you did today. You can't get Adrian back, so you'll at least make sure of Carlos."

Margaret was silent for a moment. "No, I think what I did today was finish up the job Adrian started, a job he was killed for. I know absolutely that two or three days from now Candovala would have called up Marissa and asked for Carlos back. I couldn't let that happen." She took a sip of water and started in on the carrots. "I have to give credit to Marissa. She's a brave woman. I'm a little worried about what Candovala might do."

"Brave?" Guyers sounded skeptical. "I think she's a lucky woman. Lucky that she won't be indicted along with her boyfriend." He shrugged. "Not my definition of bravery. Now, as for Margaret Binton . . . that's another story. You weren't even involved and here you are going into strange bars." He reached a hand out and patted hers. "I have great admiration for you, my dear, great admiration."

Margaret smiled. "But how's that going to effect my grade?" she asked.

"Grade?" He looked nonplussed. "Can you believe it? I've actually quite forgotten our academic association."

"Absentminded professor," she said with a grin, and

poured some coffee into their cups. "What do you think will happen now, I mean about Carlos?" she said.

He took a sip of his coffee. "Family court will hear the case sometime this week. It's in their purview to either remand the boy back to his father or to foster care. I tend to disagree with you. I would be shocked if Candovala got his son back within the next year."

"I hope you're right. And Candovala?"

"Depends. Maybe a criminal indictment for abuse. Maybe a slap on the wrist. I'm not an expert in family court matters, Margaret, but in either case, I don't think he'll suffer too much. After all, Carlos is still alive, apparently happy, at least, from what I saw. I hope Marissa is right and there won't be any permanent scarring."

"On his body, you mean?"

Guyers nodded. "Yes. Psychologically there is, no doubt, much damage. But a jury doesn't see that. And if we got a real judge, you know what I mean, Candovala might even lose his son permanently. So there's much to hope for."

"Is there anything we can do?" Margaret asked.

"Just wait. Westgate said he would call."

"I hate waiting," she said. "It's against my nature. It should be against anyone's nature over the age of seventy."

"Why, Margaret," Professor Guyers said, "you don't look a day over sixty-five."

"Imagine that," she said. "And I wasn't even fishing."

# 36

Westgate called two days later and told Margaret that Carlos was in a foster home in Queens under an emergency placement. The family had two other foster children and were delighted to be able to help their new charge. Westgate assured her that it was a loving family and that Carlos was in good hands. That was the good news. The bad news was that any court activity had been postponed until after Juan Candovala could arrange for a lawyer. That might take another week at the very least, and the initial court appearance would be only the first of many before some permanent disposition was determined.

"Just don't get your hopes up," Westgate had said. "There won't be some quick solution here. Candovala has not even been brought up on charges yet."

"What are they waiting for?" Margaret asked in amazement.

"These things take time," he said, and rung off.

So there was to be more waiting. At least little Carlos was safe. Margaret went back to her old routine of visits to the

187

Florence E. Bliss Senior Citizens Center in the morning, and warm sunny afternoons on the Broadway benches. In the evenings she watched a little television and studied for her ethics class. She saw all of her friends, who were curious as to what was happening with Mr. Lavin's murder, but as she had nothing to report, after a while they went on to other topics. She kept her weekly appointments, her shopping at Fairway, her Cub Scouts with Peter Frangapani, and her volunteer book cart work at Metropolitan Hospital. Just her normal routine, all the time waiting for the other shoe to drop, for a call from Westgate telling her to appear at family court to be a witness. She tried, as best as she could, to fill her days so she wouldn't have to concentrate on the fact that Adrian Lavin was dead, and that she knew who had killed him, and that all they could hope for was an indictment on child abuse.

On Friday night of the second week she got a call from Westgate telling her that there would be a hearing the next Monday at family court, the severe black granite edifice down at 60 Lafayette Street. Margaret made sure to wake up in plenty of time to get downtown, to a location in the city she hadn't travelled to for over thirty years since she last got a driver's licence. The hearing was scheduled for 10:00 A.M., but it was after 2:30 before all the parties were ushered into the courtroom. Margaret had asked Berdie to accompany her to help negotiate the subways, but she was not allowed into the chamber with Margaret due to the confidentiality of the proceedings. Professor Guyers was busy teaching a class, or else he would have also been there. Besides Margaret, there was Marissa, Candovala, Westgate, a lawyer for Candovala and one for the city, a clerk, stenographer, the judge, and two court officers to insure that tempers stayed calm. The door slammed shut on this entourage of eleven people, all assembled to determine what was best for little Carlos.

Candovala was dressed in a close-fitting blue suit and a white shirt, the model of paternal propriety. His answers were short and precise, and he was especially polite to the judge who directed the questioning. Throughout he kept his eyes mostly averted from those around him, but on one occasion Margaret caught him looking at her. There was something behind his eyes that made her cringe, a look of real hatred. But a second later it was gone and he was once again facing the judge.

After a few minutes she was asked to give her version of what she knew. She spoke about the druggist and also about her briefly getting a glimpse down Carlos's neck at the marks. The judge thanked her and then went on to Westgate. The caseworker read from a medical report on little Carlos that had been taken a few days after he was placed in foster care. The discolorations on his body at that point had become faint and had lost their well-defined shape. They numbered about eight, were mostly around his upper torso, and were not going to cause permanent scarring. They were from blistering, possibly but not definitely from burns. Other than that, Carlos was found to be in excellent health.

Finally Marissa was called up to tell the judge what she knew. Margaret was expecting a strong indictment on her part of Candovala, but from the very first question, Margaret sensed that the woman had decided to tone down her comments. Juan had gotten to her somehow. Money, threats? Something had happened to change her from the convinced woman she had been in her apartment to the indecisive witness testifying today. She told the judge that only once had she noticed anything on Carlos that might indicate he had been disciplined, and she had spoken to Candovala about it then. Most of the time, she claimed, Candovala was a good father and took good care of his son. She had never actually seen him raise a hand to hurt him. Carlos was, when he came to visit her, a happy child who enjoyed playing with her neighbor's children and watching television. Margaret shook her head in disbelief.

The lawyers then spoke and argued their positions. The city argued for remanding Carlos into foster care for at least one year and possibly initiating the withdrawal of parental rights. Candovala's lawyer argued for an immediate return of the child to his client. At no point was anything mentioned about bringing Candovala up on charges of child abuse. Perhaps that would come at a later date.

The judge who had to sort this all out looked down from his high bench with dispassion. He heard perhaps two dozen similar cases a day and had to, within the space of twenty minutes, make a decision that often affected lives in very significant and permanent ways. Most judges postponed major decisions as long as possible, relying on the healing effect of time. So it was with the white hair who presided over Candovala and son. He decided to decide at a later date, and told everyone to come back in two months' time. In the meantime, he was requiring Candovala to seek family counseling, keeping Carlos with his foster family, and suggesting to Westgate that some appropriate visiting schedule be set up for the two of them. Margaret could not believe her ears. Even the surrounding polished wood panelling and marble floors did not intimidate her enough to keep silent.

"Judge, he took red hot metal wire to his son and you're talking about visiting rights? You've got to be kidding."

The judge turned his stony gaze down at her. "I would like to remind you, madam, that you are here at the behest of the court, and that you are here only to give testimony as to what you know. Opinions I can get from anyone outside these doors and are, for that reason, to be kept there." He looked over the assembled group with a scowl and then, turning to his clerk, said, "What's next?"

One of the court officers went and opened the door, and the other one ushered everyone out. Westgate trailed behind Margaret who, herself, was behind Candovala. They weren't more than ten feet into the next room when Candovala turned around, and with a look of intense hatred, blurted out, "You took my kid away, you old bitch. But you'll get yours." He took a step towards Margaret, but an officer stepped between them before anything could happen. Westgate also stepped around Margaret and made sure Candovala wasn't going to do something foolish with his hands. But they couldn't stop his mouth.

"I heard how you leaned on Marissa," he shouted. "You're dead meat now. I'll find you." The officer hustled him out, but not before he gave Margaret one more searing look. Then he grabbed Marissa by the arm and walked away.

"Don't worry," Westgate said. "They all get emotional at family court. That's why they check for guns at the entrance."

"Guns?" Margaret could feel her knees weaken.

"But you don't have to worry. Everything here is confidential. It's a hearing, not a trial, so everything is sealed, including your name and address."

"Small consolation." She waved at Berdie, who was sitting patiently in the waiting room and who now got up and came over.

"Why do you think Marissa changed her mind?" Margaret asked Westgate. "If only she had given stronger testimony."

Westgate shrugged. "You can never figure these things out. I've been in situations where husband and wife are screaming at each other in front of the judge, and then leave hand in hand. But one thing I know, you always got to look for the money. Even when it's a mother crying her eyes out to get her little baby back. With Candovala too. Why do you think he's so anxious to get Carlos? So he can baby-sit him in the evenings? Uh-unh, more than likely it's the money. There's Aid to Dependent Children payments, welfare, medical, dental, food stamps, on and on. Without Carlos, Candovala is adrift like any working slob. With him, he's got the city and state as godparents. That's what it's about—the kids are just tokens." He shook his head as Berdie walked up. "You ladies going back uptown?"

Margaret nodded.

"Good, I'll give you a lift. I got my car."

"That was Candovala?" Berdie asked. "The guy that almost hit you?" She looked uneasy.

191

"That was him."

"Thank God you got a car then," she said to Westgate. "I wouldn't want to be on the streets with him out there waiting."

"That'll blow over, you'll see," the tall black man said. "They never remember."

# 37

Margaret went through a whole pack of cigarettes that evening, and a crossword-puzzle book she was saving for special occasions. Every little noise in the apartment, things she had lived with for years, now took on more sinister overtones. The refrigerator kicking in, the elevator stopping on her floor, the neighbor's kids playing with their toys above her head, all made her stop and listen intently. She knew exactly how Adrian must have felt that night she had called him. There was panic in everything that moved. She went to bed early and still had visions of Candovala's face sneering over her prostrate and bleeding body. Finally, exhausted, at midnight she fell asleep.

In the morning she felt a little better, and after drinking her coffee in the well-lit kitchen, she felt almost back to normal. The Upper West Side was a big place. How could he find one senior citizen out of thousands? She convinced herself that it was unlikely. Today was Tuesday. So she'd go shopping, which she hadn't done the day before, and at three, pick Peter Frangapani up at school for Cub Scouts. She wasn't going to let someone else dictate how she was going to live her life. In between she'd go to the Center and see who was there. Maybe she'd even have lunch out at the coffee shop. That would certainly take her mind off things. Maybe Rena could join her. She looked out the window and saw that it was threatening rain. That wouldn't stop her, she'd take her umbrella.

Three o'clock came around and found Margaret waiting inside the entrance of P.S. 142 on Columbus and Eighty-fourth Street. She was waiting there with all the other mothers and picker-uppers, trying to get in out of the slight drizzle that had been falling since noon. Peter's smiling face greeted her as always. He had his Cub Scout hat, bandana, and shirt on, and his regular school shirt in a bag. He was so proud of that Cub Scouts shirt with all its insignia, his first badges of accomplishment. Margaret had no idea what they meant, but she knew that it would have been harder to disrobe a nun on Forty-second Street than to get Peter to go to Cub Scouts without the shirt. She grabbed his hand, and together they walked to the church basement where the Cub Scouts met every Tuesday.

The meeting usually lasted for an hour-and-a-half in the large downstairs room. What mysteries took place there Margaret got secondhand, since only the boys were allowed inside. Parents, baby-sitters, siblings, and all hangers-on had to wait upstairs in a small room that doubled for a community meeting room. During that interval, many parents went back home, but Margaret had always stayed and read a book, or chatted with whomever she found there. Today the pickings were slim. One young woman had her head buried in a home-study course on hair design, and one older black lady had her eyes closed and was enjoying probably the first rest of the day. Margaret reached into her big handbag, got out her latest Robertson Davies novel, put her feet up on a nearby chair, and spent the rest of the time engrossed. An hour and a half later, Peter bubbled up from downstairs and tapped her on the shoulder.

"Wanna see a square knot?" he asked enthusiastically. Margaret nodded and in fifteen seconds, he had a short piece of rope tied into a loop with a small knot at its end. "Learned that today," he said proudly. "Wait until I show Mom." He stuck the rope in his pocket, but a little of it still hung out. "Let's go."

As soon as they hit the pavement and the noises of the city enfolded them, Margaret's nervous feeling of the day before came back. But this time it was more palpable. There was something nagging at her, and it wasn't the falling mist. Finally she stopped the boy and drew him under the umbrella.

"What is it?" he asked.

"I'm so stupid," she said, and looked behind her. Hadn't she told Candovala she went every Tuesday to Cub Scouts? How many Cub Scout meeting places were there on the Upper West Side? She looked carefully now at all the people on the block behind her, and all the people across the street, but Candovala was not one of them.

"Come on," she said to Peter. "We have to hurry."

"I'm tired," came his reply.

Was she being unreasonable? Maybe Candovala had forgotten his threat. Maybe he had forgotten her visit, her discussion of Cub Scouts. "You can rest at home," Margaret said, and started off again trying to juggle the umbrella, her handbag, and Peter's hand all at the same time.

"What's the rush?" he squeaked.

They swept around the corner and arrived on Central Park West and Eighty-eighth Street heading south. Across from them Central Park beckoned, but because of the drizzle, few people were sightseeing its newly budding trees. Margaret's eyes darted everywhere, but she still couldn't spot him. They walked quickly and covered the next block in under a minute. At Eighty-seventh Street she started to feel more relieved. This was crazy, she told herself; he was probably still at his job at the muffler shop. And then she saw a taxi swerve to pull up at the curb fifty feet behind them. She stopped long enough to get a glance at the body emerging. It was Candovala, who was now starting down the block behind them. He had been in the cab the whole time, trailing them. Then why had he gotten out? She looked ahead and spotted the subway station on Eighty-sixth. Afraid he'd lose us in the subway, she thought, that's why. Which meant he had no idea of where we live. If he had, he would know it was only a few more blocks home. She looked behind her again, and this time their eyes met, and a smile crossed Candovala's features. He wanted her to see him. He wanted her scared. He was enjoying this.

Margaret turned forward again and kept walking. Even with all the people around who might be witnesses, she thought he might do something and walk away unspotted in the confusion that followed. She felt a crawling sensation between her shoulder blades. What should she do, run? That was a joke, especially with a little boy in tow. Look for a policeman? On a rainy day, that was even funnier. And if she found one, what would she tell him? This man wants to kill me? Since when was it illegal to walk down the streets behind someone? And Candovala could just stay out of sight until the policeman got tired of the game. This thinking was getting her nowhere fast, but her walking had brought them to the subway entrance. Instinctively she tugged on Peter and headed down the stairs. If Candovala was afraid of our being in the subway, she thought, then that's just where we should go. Peter, a boy with enough street smarts to know that he never took the subway home from Cub Scouts, asked what they were doing.

"It's a little detour," Margaret said, and, closing her umbrella, put a token in the machine. A train was just pulling out of the northbound station as they got onto that platform. Office workers were walking out of the station while some kids were filing in. Shortly there were about half-a-dozen people near her on the platform as she moved slowly away from the entrance to her left, uptown. She kept her eyes glued to the stairway where Candovala would appear, and in about twenty seconds she saw him slowly descend. He paid, then walked onto their platform about thirty feet away and leaned leisurely against one of the metal columns. It was possible he was just following her to see where she lived. That would give him an opportunity to do something later when there weren't so many people around. But what if he was crazy enough to try something right here? She heard a rumbling down the track, and in a few seconds another local train shot into the station and opened its doors. The little boy by her side instinctively waited until Margaret moved, and when she did, he followed. They both took a step inside and waited by the door, and then, just as the alarm bell announced the closing of the doors, Margaret yanked him outside. It was a dangerous move, one that Margaret would never have done under other circumstances. But they both made it back safely onto the platform. The train pulled out of the station and Margaret looked for Candovala through the windows of the car. But he was not there; he was still thirty feet away back by the metal column. They were now alone on the platform, and he levered himself off and started walking their way.

"Nice try, old lady," Candovala said menacingly when he was only a short distance away. "But I seen that movie too. All I need now is a little push."

Margaret moved closer to the wall, right next to one of the few benches in the station.

"In front of this child, that's very brave," Margaret said. She had no idea how she had the nerve to talk back to him.

"What's he saying?" Peter asked with a frightened tone in his voice. "What push?"

"Don't worry, Peter, this man won't hurt you."

"I remember him, he's Carlos's dad," Peter said. "We went to visit them."

Margaret stiffened as she noticed Candovala's eyes narrow. God no, not little Peter also.

"Good memory the kid has," Candovala said. There was silence in the airless space for a few seconds as Candovala took the final steps closer.

"You killed Adrian Lavin, didn't you?" Margaret asked quickly. "You killed him because he was going to do what I did, take Carlos away."

Candovala nodded slowly. "And look where he is. And he didn't even get as far as family court."

An express train screeched through the station on the far track and the noise made Candovala look up for a moment. He was between Margaret and the token booth and entrance. If Margaret tried to run past him for help, a little trip would put her at the edge of the platform. She stood her ground and saw finally, at the turnstiles where she had entered, a few more people filtering onto the uptown platform. Candovala turned back and reached out. In that moment, Margaret dropped her umbrella and handbag and grabbed the little loop of rope sticking out of Peter's pocket, the one he had used to demonstrate his square knot. In one motion she flipped it over a projection on the back of the bench, cinching it tight. Her other hand was firmly locked around Peter's. Candovala immediately saw the problem. Unless he was willing to wrestle with her or pull the bench to the edge of the platform, it was not going to be easy to push them over. And now he heard other footsteps approaching.

He looked at her for a moment, scowled angrily, then sat down on the bench. In the next few minutes, the platform filled with enough people to make Margaret feel secure. She put the rope back and retrieved her bag and umbrella. Another train would be coming; if they didn't get on it, they'd be alone again with Candovala on an empty platform. But what were their chances on a train going uptown, away from where they lived? It was better for them to take their chances on the street. She started walking, but this time away from Candovala to the end of the platform. There she had spotted an unmanned exit to Eighty-eighth Street with one of those revolving doors made out of steel bars. As she approached it an idea, a crazy idea, jumped into her head. They stopped where the last of the people were waiting for the next train, still twenty feet away from the turngate. Margaret hesitated, looked down at Peter, then back at Candovala who was now following behind, about eight feet away. Yes, maybe it would work, she thought. The sound of another train entering the station reached her ears, and she realized she had to make a decision: the street or the train? The first car passed them and slowed to a stop, and as it did, Margaret hurried quickly for the exit, pulling Peter behind her.

She pushed Peter through ahead of her, then followed in the next section of enclosed gate. Candovala was right behind them. But before Margaret emerged, she quickly hung the curved handle of her umbrella on the outer edge of one of the stationary cross bars. She turned around, waiting to see if Candovala would follow them through the turnstile. He was there within a few seconds, not wanting to let the departing passengers ahead of him through the gate. He went so quickly that he didn't notice the umbrella that was now hanging down vertically, waiting to block the next section of bars from swinging through. When Candovala entered the compartment and advanced the gate, the umbrella caught on the moving interjecting steel bars and kept them from turning further. Too late, Candovala realized that he was trapped in a little wedge-shaped cage, unable to go back because the gate was on a ratchet mechanism to keep fare cheats out, unable to go forward because of the sturdy umbrella. He couldn't even reach the umbrella, since it was diagonally across from his compartment, about four feet away. He stuck his arm through the narrow bars as far as he could, but his fingers were still over a foot away. Then he rattled the steel bars in front of him hard, but the damp umbrella held firmly. Margaret gave a broad smile, grabbed Peter's hand once again, and the two of them went trundling up the stairs. Behind them they heard angry voices telling Candovala to get going, and a loud curse from Candovala himself. By the time someone on the inside threaded an arm through the narrow comb of steel bars and worked the umbrella free, Margaret and Peter had found a taxicab and were already three blocks away.

"You lost your umbrella," he said.

"I'll buy another," she answered.

The little boy frowned. "Was that man chasing us? He looked angry."

"No, Peter, it was just a game." She leaned back in the seat and breathed heavily. "But I think next week you will have to find someone else to take you home from Cub Scouts."

"Why, Margaret?" he asked. "You're always so much fun."

# 38

"Intolerable, that's what it is, and I've got to do something about it. Simply intolerable!" Margaret looked from one of her friends to another crammed into her small living room. She had called everyone there except Rose and Roosa, who were never near a phone. The others, six in all, were waiting patiently to hear just what had gotten Margaret worked up so much. It was, after all, 8:00, an unusually late hour in the evening for such meetings.

"Perhaps you'd like to explain," Sid finally said. "What are we talking about here? The price of a pot roast sandwich at Fine and Shapiro's? You want intolerable, how about the seven bucks to see some lousy movie."

"I am not talking minor inconvenience, Mr. Rossman," she said icily, "I'm talking about murder, or rather, attempted murder. And when the victim turns out to be oneself, the inconveniences of inflation pale by comparison. Someone tried to kill me today, and will continue to try until he succeeds. What I had hoped was an idle threat turned out to be far more sinister."

Berdie's eyes opened wide. "That guy, Candovala?"

Margaret nodded, then explained as briefly as she could the afternoon escape with Peter. The other people in the room listened intently, and when she was finished, sat there shaking their heads.

"Good Lord, Margaret, what are you going to do?" asked Rena. "I mean, this is serious."

"Indeed," Margaret said, "and requires serious counter-measures. This man has already killed once. He as much as confessed Lavin's murder to me. I feel no guilt bringing him to justice any way I can." She looked around. "Now, I've been thinking. All afternoon since I got home, I've been turning things over, and now I have a plan. But I need your help."

There was another silence in the room until Pancher asked, "Is it dangerous?"

"Not really, not unless we're incredibly unlucky," Margaret said. "But it requires some financial sacrifice and some good acting ability."

"Count me out," Berdie said. "I get hives when it's my turn to order at Zabar's. Shouting in front of all those people."

"No, you're important to this plan," Margaret said. "Besides me, you're the only one who knows what Candovala looks like."

"Just my luck," she groaned.

"Me, you count in too," Pancher said. "You need help, I give it."

"Sure," Durso said. "I need some excitement in my life. Things have been real dull since we stopped canvassing."

Rena and Sid also agreed. Margaret sat back and closed her eyes for a moment.

"What do you want us to do?" Pancher asked.

"Three things," Margaret said, reopening her eyes. "First of all, I need all the money Sid won for us, minus your original loan, that is. Fourteen hundred dollars should be enough for what I need to buy. I'm sorry, but the way I figure it, easy come, easy go. I hope you still have it. Give the money to Pancher, and when it's all there, Pancher," she looked closely at him, "I'll tell what you have to do with it."

He nodded.

"Second, I need Candovala's apartment watched before and after work. When he leaves with one particular item, I want to know about it immediately. And third, and this is the acting part, I need three of you to be ready, on a moment's notice, to each do a bag of laundry." She looked around at the staring faces and smiled innocently.

"You'd better explain," Sid said. "This is not sounding like a Sunday walk in the park."

"Of course not," Margaret answered. "Since when do you bring a murderer to justice on a pleasant Sunday outing?" She leaned closer and winked. "The best part of this whole plan is that I get to buy myself a dozen long-stem roses. I've never done that before. Now here's the deal. I want to make sure we all agree. . . ."

# 39

For five days nothing happened. Margaret had made arrangements for Peter to be taken to Cub Scouts by someone else, just in case the waiting period lasted more than a week. During that time, she did not venture farther than the corner news seller for her paper and cigarettes, which she was now buying two packs at a time. The Smoke Stoppers program was just a bad memory as far as she was concerned, bad because it had brought her into this mess in the first place, and bad because it hadn't even worked. The news seller, an older Pakistani neighborhood fixture, clucked his tongue a few mornings when she started back in on two packs, but then gave up after he tired of the game.

Berdie, Roosa, Rose, and Pancher were on the surveillance team Margaret had set up, and Rena, Sid, and Durso were on the laundry team. The first day on the job, Berdie, who had seen Candovala at the family court hearing, pointed him out to the others on her team. From then on they watched individually. The details had been worked out as carefully as if they were on a military operation inside enemy territory.

It was a difficult week for everyone. When Candovala was not working at the muffler shop, the laundry team had to drop what they were doing and wait by their bag of dirty laundry for Margaret's signal. The surveillance team had to take turns in what was becoming a damper-than-normal May. After five days, the wait became increasingly taxing.

Professor Guyers had not been there for the planning session by design, and when he subsequently asked what was happening, Margaret was just as vague. The last thing she wanted was to get her teacher and friend in trouble where he might be disbarred. As far as he knew, everything was on hold: Carlos was with the foster family, Candovala was being investigated for child abuse, and Margaret was enjoying her friends at the Florence E. Bliss Senior Citizens Center. The fact that she missed her class on ethics one night prompted him to phone, but when Margaret confessed to having a sore throat, he was mollified.

More waiting. Saturday and Sunday were difficult because Candovala was in and out all day, so they broke it into three-hour shifts. But the laundry team saw little daylight. By Monday Margaret detected some grumbling in the ranks, but she knew something had to happen soon.

When Candovala moved, they almost missed it. Berdie was paying attention to a particularly attractive pigeon with an amber-flecked pattern on his wings, when Candovala emerged from his building carrying a large bag over his shoulder. She glanced up just a few seconds before he turned the corner. Luckily, she caught his profile, saw what he was holding, and rushed to a nearby phone booth.

There was only one Laundromat in the direction he had taken. Margaret immediately called Rena, Sid, and Durso and alerted them, while Berdie continued following behind Candovala. He turned into He Ching's coin-op Laundromat, unpacked his bag of soiled clothes, stuck them in one of the larger machines, poured some Tide into the dispenser, and sat back to wait. Ten minutes later Sid entered, and then a few minutes later, Durso, and they both loaded bags of laundry in adjacent machines. The place was moderately busy; there were a few mothers with young children, one Chinese woman who seemed to be an employee, and several older people. The fluorescent light made everything brighter than needed to be, and the sounds of churning machines kept conversations to a minimum. Mostly, everyone read newspapers or books. Sid got up, walked to the window to look out, and on the way back, dropped his copy of the *Daily News* unobtrusively next to Candovala's seat. A moment later, Durso got up, passed behind Candovala to get the paper just left, and by accident knocked his box of soap powder over. He said "excuse me" to an indifferent Candovala, and set it upright again.

A minute later Rena passed by the window outside, peered in Candovala's direction, looked over at where Durso's hand was placed on the newspaper, and kept walking. So far, so good. She had noted the brand of detergent and how much was still inside. Soon the fun would begin. The two friends were sitting a few chairs apart, neither looking at each other. Durso continued to read the paper, while Sid just seemed to be looking off into space. Time passed slowly, people came and left, and finally, after half an hour, Candovala's load was done. He got up and switched it to a nearby dryer. Rena entered carrying a paper bag and a small bag of laundry in her gloved hands. She stuck her clothes in a machine, poured some of her own Tide into the dispenser, and sat down. Three minutes later Sid's load was finished, and almost immediately afterwards, Durso's machine buzzed the end of his cycle. Both men got up and started pulling out socks and shirts and transferring them to nearby dryers. Candovala merely glanced over their way, then went back to what he was reading.

"Excuse me, that's my sock you're putting into your machine," Sid said loudly. "That one over there."

206

"The white one with the blue ribbing? No it's not, it's mine," Durso answered. "Got it last year at Conway's."

"Yeah, maybe you got something like it last year at Conway's, but I got that one this year at Macy's." Sid pointed. "Give it back. I only got four pairs. See look, here's the mate."

"Yeah, and what's this?" Durso said, now raising his own voice. He too was holding up another white sock with blue ribbing. "You only got four pairs trying for a fifth." He put the questioned sock into his machine with a flourish.

"Damn it, that's mine," Sid barked and pushed Durso to the side. He reached in and plucked out the sock.

"You can't do that," Durso said, and pushed back, snatching onto the dangling sock with his other hand. Now the sock was being stretched by the two men tugging in opposite directions as though they were at summer camp in the finals of color war.

"Son of a bitch, give me that," one said.

"Go to hell!" the other replied.

Candovala got up and walked over. "Hey, calm down, guys," he said. "For Christ sakes, it's only a sock." While he was facing the two men, his back was turned on Rena as she casually got up and walked to check on her machine. As she passed by Candovala's seat she dipped at the waist for an instant, then quickly kept walking. After looking at the timer on her machine she went back to her seat.

"Tell you what," Sid said. "Let's flip for it." He reached into his pants pocket for a coin. "Heads it's yours, tails it's mine." Durso gave him a frown but finally nodded. "Here, you hold this," Sid said, and gave the damp sock to Candovala. He flipped the coin, and when he showed the result, Durso smiled.

"Mine, as it was all along. I'll take that," he said, and got the sock from the younger man. The three men broke apart and each went back to what they had been doing before the fracas began.

A half hour later, Candovala was the first to go, bundling

all his fresh laundry into his laundry bag with his box of detergent and magazine. The others left separately after their own laundry loads were done. Rena, the last to go, put her still somewhat damp clothes into her bag, slung it over her shoulder, and hurried out. She couldn't wait to get back to Margaret's apartment and report her success. After all, hadn't she been the prime player?

Switching the Tide boxes. Now that had taken some real nerve.

# 40

The following day Margaret didn't dare go in to see Morley. She sent Sid instead. Of all of her friends, Sid would be the most convincing in this vital, last part of their plan. Before he left, Margaret gave him the little vial she had saved from the roses, prepared in just the way she wanted. Then she went and waited patiently on the benches with her friends for Sid to return.

The weather had finally turned clear and warm, and the old-timers chatted amiably about a lot of different concerns, trying to take their minds off waiting for Sid. They were debating the issue of aspirin versus ibuprofen for arthritis, when Rena shouted out with a muffled cry, "Here's Sid!" and everyone held their breath.

Sid, the old gambler, was poker-faced as he wedged in between Pancher and Durso. He slowly stretched his legs, leaned back, and said how nice it was to have a little warm weather at last.

"Come on, Sidney Rossman," Margaret fumed. "What happened?"

He smiled, sat back up and nodded. "Never have I seen anyone quite so responsive. He snatched it right up."

"The whole story?" Margaret asked.

"Hook, line, and stinker." Sid looked around for their response, but everyone was too intent to be sidetracked by a simple pun. They were all leaning forward, waiting to hear. "I walked in and asked to see Morley, just like you told me. Told them I had seen something important that he might be interested in. Then I showed them the used bullet-shaped florist vial. Got me right in."

"I thought it would," Margaret said.

"Morley took one look and called some flunky in to get the thing analyzed."

"Well, they don't have to be very good to know that the powder on the inside is two grams of cocaine." She turned to Pancher. "Isn't that what you bought from that artist, Lorenzo Tyler?" The ex-janitor nodded.

"Fourteen hundred dollars' worth, just like you said. It came to fifteen grams."

"And the powder on the outside?" Margaret asked of Sid. "Did you tell them?"

"I did. I told him it smelled like detergent."

"Tide, to be exact," Rena said proudly. "I rubbed it in there myself."

"Good," Margaret said. "That will get the action rolling."

"You bet it will. Morley asked me where I found it, and when I told him I saw some guy bury it surreptitiously near a tree on Ninety-ninth Street, then described Candovala, and told him which building he went into afterwards, I thought he was ready to give me an honorary membership to the PBA."

"He didn't recognize you, did he?" Margaret asked. "I mean as being one of my friends."

Sid shook his head. "Not that I could tell. He didn't say anything. Just told me that he would handle it from here." He chuckled. "Got to hand it to you all right. I wouldn't want

210

to be Candovala when they trace down his description, then search his apartment and the Tide box, and find all those funny florist vials with the other thirteen grams of cocaine. I'd love to see the look on his face. Especially with his fingerprints being the only one on the box." Sid laughed. "You really stuck it to him, Margaret."

"Well, I suppose it's the flip side of live and let live; sin and be sinned against," Margaret said. "I don't feel particularly proud, just relieved Mr. Candovala won't be chasing me for a long, long while. And also that he won't be around to abuse his son until Carlos is old and large enough to protect himself." She smiled faintly. "I also couldn't let him get away scot-free with Adrian's murder. Besides, it was the only thing I could think of. What did Detective Green say, 'Sometimes a good solid drug arrest pulls more time than a plea-bargained murder conviction.' Especially a repeat offense like in Candovala's case. With more than five grams, up to twenty years. I checked. He'll have to live doing the time if not the crime." She smiled at her friends. "And ethically, there's precedent. I learned that in *Nix versus Whiteside*." She shrugged. "At least I think that applies. But you remember, we voted on this, and we all agreed." She looked around. "Any regrets?"

No one spoke. The noise of cars whizzing by was the only sound filling their tiny space as the eight friends sat back and regarded their small, circumscribed island on Broadway. After a few minutes, Berdie cleared her throat.

"With the nice weather, I suppose the pigeons will be coming back. I should go back home and get some crumbs."

"That would be nice," Margaret said, and opened her handbag.

"Looking for a cigarette?" Sid asked with a grin.

"No," Margaret said. "I'm still trying to cut down. Tomorrow I start my acupuncture." She shook her head resignedly. "I was really looking for the NYU summer catalog," she continued. "I think I'm going to take another course starting in June."

211

"Ethics again?" Rena asked.

Margaret frowned. "Now why would I do that?" she asked. "You think I'm going to flunk?"

After some hesitation, Sid said, "On the contrary, I think you should get an A."

"Undoubtedly," Durso agreed, and they all watched as Berdie got up and went in search of some bread crumbs for her birds.